Assessing Mr. Darcy

Assessing Mr. Darcy

A Pride and Prejudice Novel

LEENIE BROWN

LEENIE B BOOKS
HALIFAX

Contents

Dedication

I have always said that stories do not truly come alive until a reader reads them. This story will be no different in that regard. However, it is special because the idea for this book came from a comment made by a reader.

Thank you, **Екатерина**, for suggesting the idea of Mr. Collins coming to live at Longbourn when he was young. I am certain that what I have written is not at all what you had envisioned, but I hope that you enjoy my take on how the addition of a Bennet *brother* might have altered the path that brought Darcy and Elizabeth together.

Dear Reader,

This novella is part of my *Dash of Darcy and Companions Story Collection*. These *Pride and Prejudice* inspired stories are quick, sweet reads designed to fit perfectly into a busy life.

Dash of Darcy titles in this collection will focus on Darcy and Elizabeth, while each *Companion Story* focuses on characters from *Pride and Prejudice* other than Darcy and Elizabeth and is a sequel to a *Dash of Darcy* story. While references will be made in the *Companion Stories* to events which happened in the previous *Dash of Darcy* story, each sequel contains a complete happily ever after for the hero and heroine.

I am delighted that you have chosen to read this *Dash of Darcy Story* and am excited to have you discover a different sort Longbourn where the heir to the estate is not a stranger but a loyal and protective older "brother." Such a change must, of course, alter the path that Elizabeth and Darcy will take to happily ever after. I hope you will enjoy their journey.

Happy Reading!

Leenie B.

Chapter 1

Elizabeth Bennet leaned against one of the oak trees that grew on the hill near the edge of Longbourn's property. Taking out her spyglass, she settled in to watch.

Overhead the brilliant reds, yellows, and oranges were still mixed with a few traces of green, and normally at this time of year, she would sit beneath one or another of these trees and attempt to paint their splendor. The feat usually ended with her applying paint to the leaves and pressing them on her paper. Her desire to capture beauty far outshone her ability. Her future home would not be filled with her own creations. Instead, she would have to rely on purchased paintings, or perhaps, she could convince her younger sister Kitty to produce a few pieces for her. Kitty was the most artistic of her four sisters.

Today, however, observing the leaves above was but a peripheral pleasure, for today, she had far more interesting things at which to peer. Netherfield had been let at last!

The grand home with its park that abutted this very edge of Longbourn's property was to welcome a young unmarried gentleman and his sisters. One sister, she had been told by her uncle was similar in age to her. It would be a pleasure to have another lady in the neighbourhood. She smiled. Especially a lady with a wealthy brother in want of a wife.

"What are you doing?"

Elizabeth jumped, nearly dropping her spyglass. "Why must you insist on startling me, William?"

William Bennet smirked. "Because it is so delightful to see you jump."

"It is because I can do sums better than you." Had Elizabeth's hair not been secured under her bonnet, it would have flipped quite satisfactorily as she turned her head.

"Yes, well, you inherited your father's keen mind, and I am stuck with my father's dull one." He stood next to her on her left and leaned against the tree trunk.

Elizabeth lifted the spyglass and looked toward

Netherfield as her heart pricked her. Finally, after no more than two minutes of silence, she turned to him. "You have had Papa to guide you, and you have done well. I should not have been so cruel as to point out something with which you struggle. But you do vex me at times. I do not appreciate having the working of my heart tested on such a regular basis simply because you are light of foot."

He shrugged. "And I should not startle you, but we both know that I will continue to tease, and you will continue to retaliate with the one thing you do better than I."

Elizabeth's brows rose. "One thing?"

He laughed. "The one thing I will allow that you do better than me."

"I dance better than you."

"Very well. I will admit that you do two things better than me, but I will not admit to anything further. A brother must feel at least marginally superior to his younger sister."

Elizabeth allowed it to be. He was not her brother by birth. He had been born William Collins, a distant cousin to her father. However, even at birth, he had been far more important to her family than just some cousin. It did not matter that her father and his father had not spoken to one another in years. William Collins was the heir to Longbourn since her father had never produced a son.

It had been years — fifteen, to be precise — since William had arrived with his few bags and his poor manners and lack of learning on Longbourn's steps. His father had died, and since there was no nearer relation, and since he was the heir to Mr. Bennet's estate, the child had been delivered with all his worldly possessions to them, to be their son and brother.

He had been ten, and after six months of living with them, he had asked if he too could be a Bennet. Her father had willingly obliged, excessively pleased to have someone bear his name who would not be giving that name away before a parson in a marriage ceremony.

A carriage approaching Netherfield, brought Elizabeth back from her reverie, and she focused her glass to look as closely at it as she could. She could not see much detail, but the equipage did appear to be very fine, almost regal.

"A carriage," she said, handing the spyglass to William.

William adjusted the glass for his use and whistled. "This Bingley fellow is not shallow in the pockets, is he?"

"I dare say he is not," Elizabeth agreed. "Give the glass back when they have stopped. I want to see how the grooms and driver tend to their passengers."

William laughed. "You do not. You wish to see if Mr. Bingley is as handsome as he is rumoured to be." He looked through the glass once more. "There is a second carriage." He handed the glass to her. "You will want to see this one."

"Why?" she asked, positioning herself to be able to look at the second carriage.

"You will know when you see it."

"Oh, my!" She looked at William. "Does Mr. Bingley have two carriages, one that is lovely and another that could carry the Prince Regent?"

William shook his head. "I would venture a guess that he has not come alone."

"A friend?"

"That would be my assumption. A very wealthy guest."

"Do you suppose it is a gentleman?"

William laughed. "Yes. A single gentleman is not going to bring some fancy lady with him."

"Why not?" Elizabeth made a face at her brother. "He has sisters. It could be a friend of theirs."

She scowled at the look of disbelief on William's face. It was his way of questioning her ability to reason things, and she hated it. Not because it was a hideous face or anything like that, but because he never used that expression except when she had not thought things through properly. She despised being wrong.

He leaned near her ear as she watched the carriages approach the house. "He could be bringing his mistress. I hear many of the wealthy men from town have them."

"Oh, for heaven's sake, William! You must stop reading the society paper and listening to Lydia. And please refrain from speaking to me of such things. They really are reprehensible. Mary is not wrong about that."

Mary, the third eldest Bennet daughter, was a very serious sort of young woman who loved nothing better than to study books of etiquette and when she had none of those, she scoured sermons. Their father teased that if Mary did not marry, she would be the most sought-after governess in all the land, for her knowledge of how a young lady should or should not present herself was of superior quality.

Lydia, the youngest Bennet, was the opposite of everything Mary was. Lydia loved to laugh and found sport in most things. She was also fond of presenting herself as a less-than-proper young lady. Elizabeth wished her father would do more to correct such behaviour, but he seemed incapable of scolding Lydia as severely as she sometimes deserved. Lydia was the baby. Lydia was young. Lydia meant no harm.

Even William tolerated Lydia's behaviour more than he should, though he, at least, would scowl before chuckling at her antics.

"Do you see Mr. Bingley?"

Elizabeth pushed him away. Or more precisely she attempted to push him away from hanging over her shoulder. But William was a large fellow, sturdy, strong, and tall. She would have had just as much hope of pushing the oak over as she had of moving William if he did not wish to be moved, and at present, he did not wish to be moved.

"Not yet."

"I will have you know that I know more about town and in what sorts of devious behavior some gentlemen participate than is found in the papers."

If Elizabeth were not so focused on not missing Mr. Bingley's arrival, she would have rolled her eyes. "Yes, I know. You learned many things at university. Not all of them useful."

He chuckled. "There you are wrong."

She turned toward him. "How is knowing about mistresses and cockfights and all the rest useful?"

"I have five sisters to see well-matched. You do not think I am going to house you all forever, do you?"

She swung her arm to her side and smacked him in the stomach with a satisfying thud.

He bent forward. "I meant to say you are all far too pretty to remain unattached."

"I thought so," Elizabeth replied. "Oh, the carriage doors are opening."

She watched as a gentleman helped a lady out of the first carriage and wrapped her arm around his. That must be the sister who was married and her husband. The gentleman who was likely Mr. Bingley exited next.

"What does he look like?"

"Very handsome." She held the glass out to William but did not let go of it. She still needed to see the other sister and whomever it was in that second coach.

William whistled.

"What?" Elizabeth pulled the glass back and looked.

"She's a beauty." There was a hint of admiration in William's voice that Elizabeth rarely heard.

"Prettier than Charlotte?"

"Yes. And stop trying to match me with your friend."

Elizabeth lifted and lowered one shoulder. "You cannot disagree that joining the prominence of our family with that of Sir Williams' would not be a good alliance."

"And are you going to marry for the advantage of the match?"

He knew perfectly well she was not. "I am not the heir. You have a duty to the estate."

"To sire a son as well as seeing that the tenants are well and my own domain does not crumble around me. That is my duty. That does not require me to marry for advantage, and if it did, Charlotte has very little money. Estates run best with funds, not titles and prestige."

Elizabeth shot him an annoyed look. "Do not forget you must take care of Mama. Charlotte gets on well with Mama, and Charlotte is very good with figures."

She knew that smirk he wore and prepared herself to hear something that would likely perturb her further.

"Yes, but I would prefer a figure like that," he pointed toward Netherfield, "and not like Miss Lucas's."

"Charlotte is pretty!"

"I did not say she was not. But she is two years older than me, and to be blunt, she dresses like a spinster."

"She does not! She likes greys and browns."

Elizabeth only received a huff in reply.

"Oh, my!" she said as the occupant of the second carriage climbed out of his equipage. "He is tall." And handsome.

"Who is?" William pulled the glass away from her. "I think I am taller."

"But not so handsome," Elizabeth teased.

"I should hope my sister does not find me overly

handsome. Just handsome enough to recommend me to her friends – both the old and new ones. You are planning to be friendly to the new neighbours, are you not?"

Elizabeth shrugged. "If they are tolerable, yes."

"They are tolerable," William insisted.

"You have not met them."

"I have seen enough to know that I wish them to be tolerable. How about you? We are still hoping Mr. Bingley will suit for Jane, are we not?"

Elizabeth nodded. "Of course, it is best if the eldest marries first. And Jane is such a sweet girl. She deserves to be happy and," she grimaced, for she knew what teasing was to follow when she added the last word, "wealthy."

William laughed heartily.

"But only if she loves him, and he loves her. I would not see Jane in a loveless marriage for all the gold in the empire," Elizabeth added quickly, speaking above the continued laughter. "She should have an army of servants to make her life easy because she is the most caring of us all."

She swung her arm again and smacked him. It was the most effective way to get him to be serious. He may not have been born to her father, and he may not have the same quick wit, but William had adopted her father's sense of humor quite readily.

"You'll never snare a husband if they find out how violent you are, Lizzy Bennet." He rubbed his abdomen. "But I agree. Jane deserves the best. You all do. You have done so much for me."

Elizabeth wrapped her arm around his. "What have we done for you?" She nodded toward the path, and they began the long walk back to Longbourn House from the oak tree.

"You took me in. You allowed me to have your name, and you have accepted me as a brother. You never treated me as less than you."

Elizabeth squeezed his arm more tightly. "How else were we to treat you? We had no attic room in which to lock you."

He chuckled. "Yes, well, I know the word is not one we use often, but I love you and Jane and Mary and Kitty and Lydia and our parents. See, you allow me to call your mother and father my mother and father. Not everyone would do that."

Elizabeth smiled up at him before resting her head against his shoulder. "Find me a gentleman as tall as you so that my head will fit just below his shoulder just as it does on you."

"And you will assist me in finding a lady to my liking?"

"Is your liking Charlotte?"

"No."

Elizabeth sighed dramatically. "I suppose, if I must." She peeked up at him again. "Miss Bingley?"

"If she is not too dreadful or already attached to that tall, handsome fellow." He nudged her with the arm she held. "If she is attached to the friend, do you think you could attempt to persuade him to like you enough to not like her?"

"If I cannot, perhaps Lydia could," Elizabeth teased. Lydia was an expert at flirting.

"No."

Elizabeth looked up at him, her brow furrowed. He never spoke so firmly about Lydia. He was more likely to give Lydia what she wished than deny it.

"She is too young," he answered her unspoken question. "She should not be properly out until next year, and even then, she will be too young." He sighed. "Some of you must marry soon. I really cannot look out for all of you and keep Lydia from destruction."

"Destruction?" The word leapt from Elizabeth's lips.

"The militia will be arriving soon."

Ah! Now, William's position made sense to Elizabeth. Lydia loved any gentleman in a fine suit of clothes who carried himself in a gallant fashion. A uniform and a soldier's swagger would be an even more tempting treat.

He blew out a breath. "But enough of that. I am still a young man. Father has not departed, and there is hope that both you and Jane will soon be wed."

"Both Jane and me?"

"Do not sound so shocked. You did call the stranger handsome, did you not?"

"Not in so many words. I said he was more handsome than you. That is not the same as saying he is handsome."

"Then you do not find him handsome?"

Elizabeth pressed her lips together.

"No reply is the same as admitting I am right," William said.

"Why must you be so frustrating?"

"Because you are so good at sums," he teased. "Now, tell me. Do you find the stranger handsome?

Should I appraise him and report to you when father and I call at Netherfield." He lowered his voice. "Do not tell Mother we intend to call. Father is enjoying his tease."

Elizabeth laughed. Her father was always enjoying a tease of her mother. "Very well. So long as you never reveal that I am amenable to receiving your report about the stranger."

"Not a word shall pass my lips."

He winked at her, and she hoped that his promise would be as sure as his promises to her usually were.

Chapter 2

Fitzwilliam Darcy blew out a breath as he exited his carriage. The quiet portion of this stay was over. Solitude would not be easy to find while he was here, and he so loved solitude. He stretched and straightened his jacket. The house appeared in good repair, and the staff seemed eager to greet them. These were all good things. Bingley just might have done well with this decision.

It was not that his friend lacked sense; he just seemed to wish to see the good in a person or situation so greatly that anything negative could be forgotten far too easily.

"What did I tell you?" Charles Bingley approached him. "It is beautiful, is it not?"

Darcy nodded. "The exterior looks very good."

"The interior is equally as lovely," Bingley assured him. "And the décor is quite tasteful. I do not think you will find a thing of which to disapprove."

"We will see the stables later?"

Bingley chuckled. "Your horses will be well-tended. I do know how to care for cattle. I just do not know how to be the master of this." He waved his hand toward the house. "Now, come. We do not want to miss Caroline's opinions."

Darcy really did not care if he heard Caroline Bingley's opinions on this house or any other. Charles's twin sister was as critical as Charles was accepting.

"Oh, Mr. Darcy!" Caroline cried as he entered. "What do you think of my brother's folly? Such a grand home in such a desolate place. Did you see the high street? One hat maker – one! And I would venture a guess that the styles are not current."

"Hats can be ordered from town," Bingley replied. "As can many other things, and it is not more than a half-day's drive to London. Therefore, there is little about which to be concerned. Indeed, your being separated from your favourite shops might just allow me to preserve the inheritance Father left me."

"Charles, do be serious," Louisa interjected.

"What sort of gentlemen might a lady such as Caroline find in this remote location?"

A small smile passed between the two sisters. Darcy knew exactly which gentleman they hoped to secure as Caroline's future mate. It was a choice of which he did not approve. No matter how pretty Caroline was or how much he liked her brother, he did not wish to marry her. She was not the sort of lady he desired – not that he had found such a lady in town, Derbyshire, or Kent.

"Most gentlemen have an estate that is not in the center of London," he said. "There may be one or two in Hertfordshire or nearby who would do quite well for Caroline." He turned away to look at a painting on the wall, so that he would not have to hide his smirk at the clucking and gasping that came from Bingley's sisters.

"Aye!" Bingley cried. "And Hurst has a townhouse from which you can conduct your search while in town."

Silently, Darcy thanked his friend for not pushing Caroline toward him.

"Are you going to remain here for the season?" Caroline asked in surprise. "How will you find a wife if you do?"

"I hear from the solicitor who arranged the lease of Netherfield that there is a family of five beautiful ladies three miles from my door." He pointed one way and then the other. "I am not certain in which direction you will find Long – something." His face scrunched. "Longburn?

"Born," Darcy muttered. "Longbourn." How many times had he heard the details of where Netherfield was located in relation to pretty ladies over the past week? It had to have been at least a dozen times. His cousin, Richard Fitzwilliam, had even expressed an interest in visiting just to see the spectacle of these renowned beauties of Hertfordshire. How Bingley had forgotten the name of the estate was beyond Darcy's capability to understand. He sighed. To be fair, the man had only mentioned the name of the estate twice.

"Right!" Bingley cried. "Longbourn! That is it!"

Bingley could not contain his smile, and Darcy knew that his friend's excitement at finally having leased an estate as his father had hoped he would was hampering the man's ability to think straight. He could not fault his friend for that.

"I do believe you promised me a tour on our arrival," Darcy suggested. "May I suggest we start with my room?" He turned to Caroline and Louisa. "You will excuse us, will you not? I am certain you will wish to refresh after your journey, and Charles will want my opinion on many things that will bore you."

"We will join you for dinner," Bingley added. Then turning to the housekeeper, he said, "My sisters will also need a tour, of course, and if you could have some sort of refreshment sent to the study... I expect Mr. Darcy and I will begin our tour there after we have seen our rooms."

"The blue bedroom has been prepared for Mr. Darcy," Mrs. Nichols replied.

"It is the third door on the left?"

"Yes, sir. That is the one." The housekeeper then turned to the Hursts and Caroline and offered to show them to their rooms and have tea set out in the drawing room in half an hour's time.

"Handily done," Bingley commented as his sisters and brother-in-law left the room.

"Thank you," Darcy replied with a grin.

"I have had my fill of Caroline's displeasure in not being consulted about the leasing of this estate. The distance to town is not far unless, of course, you must travel it with an unhappy sister."

Darcy chuckled. "I can understand that. Georgiana is not so vocal as Caroline, but she is not backward in making her displeasure known. A trip from town to Derbyshire can be harrowing if she is put out with me – which she seems to be more and more often." Their recent trip from Ramsgate to London had been excruciating.

His aunt had assured him it was due to her age and that this stage would pass eventually or if not, his uncle had added, Georgiana would soon enough be *properly* wed, and then it would fall to someone else to weather her ups and downs. His sister's marrying, however, was not something Darcy wished to contemplate. He had come perilously close to losing her to a scoundrel recently, and his uncle and his aunt knew it. It was why she was staying with them currently while he was in Hertfordshire. Mrs. Annesley, her new companion, seemed better than the previous one, but neither Darcy nor his cousin Richard, who was co-guardian of Georgiana, wished to rely entirely on their own opinions. Therefore, Lord and Lady Matlock were enlisted to act as observers for the time being.

"I would like to take a ride around the estate at

some point," Darcy said as they began their ascent of the stairs. "Tomorrow morning might be soon enough unless you care for an escape before dinner?"

Bingley chuckled. "We must inspect the stables, so a short ride would not be unwelcome." He smiled. "Especially if it is in the direction of Longbourn."

Darcy shook his head. "Wait until the father calls on you before you introduce yourself to any of his daughters."

"There are five daughters," Bingley continued as if Darcy had not tried to dissuade him from the topic. "We could be brothers if we were each to find one to our liking."

"We could be brothers if you would marry Georgiana as your sister wishes," Darcy whispered.

"Or if you married Caroline as my sister wishes," Bingley replied. "I think we both would desire to become brothers in a different fashion."

Darcy shrugged. "At least with you, I would not need to worry about Georgie."

"She has no interest in me," Bingley opened the door to the blue bedroom. "And I have no interest of that sort in her. I would prefer a more mature lady. One who is steady and calm – not that Georgiana is not those things, but she is young and..."

"Say no more," Darcy interrupted. "It is just now, after what happened in Ramsgate, that I find I would like to know she is being cared for by someone as honorable as you are, and since she seems to find me such a bore and rigid, you seemed the perfect sort of fellow."

Bingley clapped him on the shoulder. "Then I shall help you find another me for her when the time comes." His lips tipped into a crooked smile. "Not that finding another like me is going to be an easy task."

Darcy laughed. "No, I would have to agree. You are a unique creation, which is why if these fabled beauties are not to your liking, I would not be opposed to your considering Georgiana."

"If all my other options fail, I will give it some thought," Bingley assured him with a laugh. "Now, you will wish to know that my room is just four doors down the hall to the right."

"And Caroline's?"

"Do you plan on visiting it?" Bingley teased.

"I wish to avoid it," Darcy replied as he rang the

bell for his man and began to strip off his travelling clothes.

"One door beyond mine," Bingley replied. "I tried to place you as far from her as I could without being too obvious in my intent." He lifted an eyebrow. "I am not the sort to push my sister at a friend."

"That is because your sister is of a marriageable age and not at all what your friend desires in a wife, and you know it. While I, on the other hand, think you and my sister would suit quite well once she is old enough. But," he held up a hand to stop Bingley's protest, "I will not push her at you. I will merely present her as an option and be happy for you if you should find another more fitting choice."

"Do you like it?"

Darcy turned to look at his friend. Confusion was written clearly in his expression. Did he like what?

"Netherfield," Bingley clarified without Darcy saying a word.

"What I have seen of it, yes."

Bingley's shoulders relaxed, and he smiled. "And the neighbourhood?"

"I have yet to meet anyone from the neighbourhood, but the town did not look so horrid as Caroline seemed to think."

"There is an assembly in two weeks. We should become acquainted with everyone by then," Bingley assured him with delight. Bingley was fond of social gatherings.

Darcy was not, and he groaned. "Everyone?"

Bingley's head bobbed up and down.

"Can I not just meet a few of the prominent men and then cast my judgment? Must I meet everyone?"

Bingley continued to nod. "And you must attend the assembly. I told them that you would."

Darcy's mouth dropped open. "You told them what? And who is them? You mentioned nothing about an assembly when you begged me to come here."

Bingley laughed. "I am not so daft as you might think, old man. What chance did I have of getting you to consent to come if I had told you?"

"None," Darcy grumbled.

"Precisely!" Bingley stood at the door. "*Them* refers to the solicitor, who is the uncle to the pretty young ladies, and Sir William. I think you will like him, although he does ramble on about some things."

If Bingley had noticed rambling enough to list it as a possible annoyance, then Darcy very much doubted he would like Sir William. He had turned to his valet to request his riding clothes but paused. "Wait. Did you just say that these ladies you hope we will find to our liking are the nieces of a country solicitor?"

Bingley shook his head. "Do you listen to yourself when you speak like that?"

"When I speak like what?"

Bingley lifted his chin and peered down his nose at Darcy while affecting a snobbish voice. "Did you say these ladies were related to a country solicitor? I should hope not. I would not wish for my clothing to be sullied with their presence."

"I am not a prig," Darcy defended.

"If you say so," Bingley replied. "But you sound like one at times."

The comment rankled. There were reasons for caution. "You should be looking to marry a gentleman's daughter. You will be a gentleman and need a wife who is familiar with the rank."

Bingley lifted an accusatory brow and shook his

head as if disappointed. "Is it impossible for a solicitor to be related to a gentleman?" he asked.

Darcy's brows knit in confusion. "Then they are gently bred ladies?"

Bingley nodded. "Longbourn is the name of an estate." He tipped his head and smirked. "Had you forgotten they live at Longbourn, the estate next to mine."

Darcy hated it when Bingley became testy in a one-who-knows-all sort of fashion, especially when it was when Darcy had made an error in reasoning. It was as if the man enjoyed pointing out Darcy's faults. He did not need Bingley to do that. He had his cousin Richard for that.

Bingley began to open the door. "I will meet you at the bottom of the stairs in a quarter hour. Perhaps we should begin by inspecting the side of the property that adjoins Longbourn's, so that you can see that it is a proper estate."

Darcy grabbed a cushion from the chair near him and hurled it at Bingley. He could hear Bingley laughing as the cushion hit the door and not its intended target.

"Shall I be ready to return to London at a moment's notice, sir?" his man asked.

Darcy shook his head. "No, not just yet. I think I can survive him for at least a while." He blew out a breath. "Even if it means attending an assembly."

"Very good, sir," his man replied. "The brown or tan breeches?"

"Tan." Fifteen minutes and then after some fortifying tea, he could be on his horse and gaining some sort of perspective on where he was and what troubles he might face during his stay at Netherfield. Nothing was so relaxing or refreshing to his mind as a ride. He sighed. Yes, a ride was just what he needed.

Chapter 3

"Are they here?" Jane asked eagerly when Elizabeth and William had returned to Longbourn's garden.

Elizabeth nodded. "And Mr. Bingley is as handsome as Uncle said he was."

"And accompanied by an equally as handsome sister," William added.

Jane chuckled as she took Williams other arm to make a turn of the garden. "Mama will not be happy to hear that. She bemoans the number of young ladies in the neighbourhood as it is."

"She'll be happier when she hears that Mr. Bingley has brought a handsome and wealthy gentleman with him," William whispered. "And he has caught the eye of our sister," he added in an even lower tone.

"William!" Elizabeth cried. "You promised to not say a word."

"You were not going to tell Jane?" William scoffed.

Elizabeth lifted her chin and did not reply. Of course, she had intended to tell Jane. She told Jane everything, for Jane was not only her eldest sister but also one of her closest friends, much like William was.

"I will not mention it to Mother or Father," William's tone was apologetic. "I promise."

"And none of our other sisters," Elizabeth added.

"It will be yours and mine and Jane's secret," William assured her. "Will you forgive me for mentioning the handsome stranger to Jane?"

"He did not mean any harm, Lizzy, and he did not tell me anything you would not have told me eventually."

It was just like Jane to attempt to make things better. She seemed to have a greater need than most to see things returned to as peaceful a state as possible. Her constancy and tranquility were something which was knit into the very fiber of her being. She could not be parted from it, and it could not be parted from her. It was her nature, and that nature was both a balm to everyone she met and the basis upon which her beauty rested.

Elizabeth shrugged. She did not wish to be done being perturbed with William, but she knew she truly had very little reason to be overly put out. "So long as he says nothing – absolutely nothing – about my finding the gentleman who accompanied Mr. Bingley handsome, I think I can overlook this small breach of his promise."

"Not a word further will fall from my lips regarding your interest in that gentleman," William said.

"Then you are forgiven."

"Lady Lucas said that Mr. Bingley has promised to attend the assembly."

Elizabeth had not heard so much excitement in Jane's voice when speaking of an assembly before. "Are you so anxious to meet him?"

"I cannot lie," Jane whispered. "I am intrigued. There are no acceptable gentlemen left in the area for me to consider, and if Papa will not send me to town for a season, I do not know where I will find a husband. Aunt and Uncle Gardiner do their best, but their soirees are not those bursting with landed gentry. And I do so wish to have an estate to call home and not just a fine house in town."

"No tradesmen for our Jane," William declared. "She is too fine a lady for that!"

"Indeed, she is," Elizabeth agreed while Jane shook her head and looked as displeased as Jane could muster when not truly put out.

"Did you walk far?" Jane asked.

"No, just to the knoll looking over Netherfield and back," Elizabeth replied. "Why?"

"I was wondering if perhaps after we have had tea with Mama and you have told her all you know..." Jane hesitated. "We could go riding."

"That is very forward of you," Elizabeth teased.

"I would just like to get a glimpse of him," Jane added. "All my hopes rest upon this Mr. Bingley, and Papa is still refusing to call on him."

"He has just arrived, Jane. Papa cannot call on him so soon."

"But will he call at all? He refuses to allow me to attend a season, and he tells Mama he will not call on the new neighbour. I am beginning to believe he wishes for me to never marry. Why else would he have refused Mr. Connor two years ago? He seemed a fine choice for a husband. He admired me, and I admired him."

"He was not what he seemed," William interjected.

"What do you mean?" Jane demanded.

"Mr. Connor and I attended school together. He had several ladies he admired and at least one he had led to believe he was going to make an offer of marriage." He looked toward the house and led them in the opposite direction. "She and her child received a small pittance from him and then nothing. She had many suitors when he met her, but now, she has no husband. She lives with a relation somewhere is what I heard."

"Can it be true?" Elizabeth could not contain her surprise. Mr. Connor had never appeared to be anything less than a perfectly honorable gentleman.

"My sources of information are good. I am sorry. It is true."

"And you never told us?" Jane asked.

"Father did not wish to cause you more pain than he knew his refusal of Mr. Connor was going to cause." He looked at Elizabeth. "I promised not to say a word, so you must not tell him that I have told you. I would hate to disappoint him, but," he stepped away from them, removed his hat, and ran a hand through his hair, "how could I not reveal what I know when Jane questions our father's intentions?"

Jane's hand lay on her heart. "Mr. Connor was so bad?"

William nodded. "He was."

"And Papa would rather I think ill of him than know the truth and feel pain?"

William shrugged. "He would do anything to see you happy."

"And these two years I have thought he did not care for my happiness. I have been so critical in my mind of everything he has done. Far more critical than I should be."

Jane looked so miserable that Elizabeth immediately wrapped her arm around her sister's shoulders while doubting that Jane's version of critical was truly as horrid as Jane seemed to think it was.

"You told Papa about Mr. Connor?" Jane asked William.

"I did."

"Thank you," Jane whispered. "I would not have wished to be tied to such a man." She looked from one to the other of her companions. "Imagine my misery if I had accepted him!"

Jane's sorrow of a moment ago was sliding into anger. Anger was something Jane was as capable of showing as Elizabeth was at times, particularly when that anger was at the perfidy of another. Jane was calm and steady, but she also desired justice.

"You must assess Mr. Bingley," Jane said to William. "You must determine if I should like him or not. And his friend, too. I would not wish for Lizzy to fall for someone like Mr. Connor."

There was an urgency to the demand, and William looked sufficiently solemn as he agreed to be their protector from all sorts of unsavoury gentlemen.

"Do you still wish to go riding?" Elizabeth asked as they turned once again toward the house.

"Oh, most certainly!" Jane cried. "You are not the only curious creature, Lizzy."

~*~*~

"And his friend has a carriage that is finer than Mr. Bingley's, you say?" Mrs. Bennet fanned herself with her handkerchief at such wonderful news. "Did he appear single?"

Elizabeth looked at William. "Did he appear single to you?" How exactly did a gentleman appear single from such a distance?

"There was no lady on his arm, and he did not look overly old." William's head bobbed from side to side as he attempted to make a calculation. He made that gesture often when he was attempting to decide between two options. "I would venture he is not yet thirty."

"Is he handsome?" Mrs. Bennet's excitement was building. Elizabeth could hear it in her voice.

The right corner of William's mouth tipped upward, causing Elizabeth to catch her breath and pray that he would not mention her.

"I am perhaps not the best judge of such things, but I think he could be considered handsome even if he did not have such a fine carriage."

Mrs. Bennet turned to Elizabeth. "Did you think he was handsome?"

"I did. Both he and Mr. Bingley were very handsome from what I could see of them through my glass."

Mrs. Bennet clapped her hands. "Two daughters married. Jane shall have her pick and then..." she looked around the room at her daughters, "one of you shall have the other."

"Elizabeth shall have the other," William inserted. "She is the second eldest, and it is the natural order of things that the older sisters should marry before the younger ones. We would not want to see any of them on the shelf, and those who are closest to such a travesty should be put forward first."

Mrs. Bennet gasped. "You are right. You are very, very right. I had not thought of it so, but Elizabeth is not getting any younger."

Elizabeth's brows furrowed in displeasure at being referred to as nearly past her prime when she was only twenty.

"And she is the most likely to pose the most problem in making a match," her mother continued.

Elizabeth gasped.

"You are so stubborn," her mother replied. "You insist on stating your own opinion on things even when it disagrees with a perfectly acceptable gentleman's opinion. That is not the best recommendation to a man that you will be a biddable wife."

"Lizzy is anything but biddable," Lydia declared, causing Kitty to titter.

"I shall be perfectly biddable for a man of sense."

"For a man who has the good sense to see things as you do," Mary muttered.

Elizabeth arched a brow at her next youngest sister. "I do believe that is what I said."

"Oh, Elizabeth," her mother cried in exasperation. "You shall never marry with such an attitude. You are altogether too headstrong. A certain amount of stubbornness is an asset to a lady, but so much is untenable. Simply untenable. If only your father had agreed with me on that, you would be as mild as Jane."

"My dear," said Mr. Bennet from behind his book, "your second daughter's temperament is such that no matter how you might have attempted to make her pliable, there was no hope of her ever being as mild as Jane. You'd have better luck attempting to make Lydia as fond of propriety as Mary."

"Papa!" Lydia cried.

"You are not always proper," her father replied. "I really ought to confine you to your room and remove your allowance more for some of your actions, but unfortunately I seem unable to do so."

"Because she would wail far too much," Mary muttered.

Her father lifted a brow and gave her a reproving look.

"I am sorry," she said.

"You are forgiven, as well as correct. I do love peace as much as Jane." And with that, he turned his attention back to his book.

That was not, however, enough to end Mrs. Bennet's discussion of the matter.

"I still believe Lizzy could be more pliable."

"She does not wish it," Mr. Bennet said without lifting his eyes. "There will be a gentleman who will appreciate her keen mind and determined spirit."

"I am certain I have never heard of such a thing," Mrs. Bennet declared.

"You oppose me quite regularly, my dear, and I still have not turned you out."

Mrs. Bennet gasped.

"Nor would I," her husband continued. "I find I like you far too well to be without you."

"I should say you do," Mrs. Bennet agreed with a little smile.

The room fell silent for a moment as the clock on the table near their father's favourite chair ticked away the time.

"Will you call on him?" It was Mrs. Bennet who broke the silence.

"Call on whom?"

Elizabeth saw the way her father's lips twitched.

"Mr. Bingley, of course!" her mother replied with some force.

"But not the handsome stranger? Shall I wait until he has departed before I call?"

"Oh, Mr. Bennet, you vex me most severely. I am certain my nerves shall see me in an early grave."

"You are far too young to worry about that," her husband replied. "Your nerves shall likely outlive both you and me."

"Mr. Bennet! Do not speak of such things, for I do not wish to think about them." Her handkerchief fluttered in front of her face more rapidly.

"I shall call on them tomorrow," Mr. Bennet said softly, and then when his wife had looked his direction in delighted surprise, he winked at her before turning his eyes back to his book once more. "But only if I can have some peace until I do."

Mrs. Bennet immediately stood. "Kitty, Lydia, go find something to do in your room. Mary," she waved her hand, "never mind, you shall not make a peep because you have your book. Jane, Lizzy – "

"Might we go riding, Mama?" Jane asked.

"Yes, I think you must," she agreed. "And I shall

see Cook about a dinner party." She turned to her husband. "You must invite them to dine with us."

"I will do no such thing."

"But your daughters." She clamped her lips closed as he raised a brow. "I shall speak to Cook to be prepared just in case you change your mind and wish to invite them to dine."

"I shall not change my mind," he replied.

Elizabeth knew he would change his mind eventually. Her father loved peace far too much to endure too many petitions from their mother.

"William will ride with us," Elizabeth said to her mother.

"Oh, that is an excellent idea." She followed them to the door, but then she turned back toward her husband. "Do you suppose you could ask what their favourite dessert might be?"

"I am not inviting them to dinner, nor am I inquiring after their likes and dislikes on such topics."

"But your daught—very well, I shall just plan on your favourite."

Their poor father. As much as her mother instructed Elizabeth on being pliable, she demonstrated quite the opposite. It was a rare discussion between her father and mother when they agreed on everything.

Jane wrapped her arm around Elizabeth's. "Come on. Before she decides she needs us to help her decide receipts." She pulled Elizabeth toward the stairs. "We will meet you at the stables, William." And with that, she dropped Elizabeth's arm and scampered up the stairs.

"She seems eager to be away," William said with a laugh.

"Indeed, she does," Elizabeth agreed before dashing up the stairs behind Jane. And who could blame her? There were handsome gentlemen just three miles away, and, to be perfectly honest, Elizabeth was just as curious to catch another glimpse of them as Jane was to get her first.

Chapter 4

Darcy had found his tea with Bingley to be refreshing, but not so refreshing as the feel of the wind against one's person as he rode. At least, that is how Darcy saw it. He and Bingley had discussed the basics about which books were most important to look over first and what Bingley's hopes were in securing an estate like Netherfield. It was for Bingley as it was for many gentlemen.

Bingley wished to gain the prominence that such an estate would bring him as well as a place into which he could put some of his inheritance in such a fashion that it would continue to reap benefits well past when he departed this earth. Bingley was no fool. He was happy and amiable as well as obliging to a fault at times, but he was no fool once he put his mind to a matter. It would take some doing, but Darcy did not expect it would be overly long before Bingley understood the workings of an estate as well as any gentleman did. Darcy smiled wryly. Bingley had the added advantage that he was likely to gain the approval of all his neighbours with very little effort. That was how Bingley was. He liked people, and they liked him. It was an enviable quality.

"I see the knoll," Bingley circled back to where Darcy was riding at a slower pace. "There." He pointed to his left. "And that fence there must be the one of which the groom spoke. We are nearly at the end of Netherfield's lands in this direction. I shall have to ask him tomorrow for a marker of where it ends in the opposite direction."

"Do you truly care to know?" Darcy teased. "Are there pretty ladies at an estate in all four directions?"

Bingley laughed. "I wish there were, but I think the only pretty ladies that are near my estate are in this direction. Mr. Philips did not mention any others."

"Mr. Philips, *their uncle*, did not tell you about any other pretty ladies? How odd." Darcy's tone was sardonic.

Again, Bingley laughed. "You should be so light-hearted more often, for you are very good at it."

"I cannot be." Darcy's reply was quick. He found it incredibly difficult to relax with anyone he had not known for any length of time. And even then, there were those such as his aunt Catherine and Caroline around whom he could only marginally relax, though he had known them for years. Lady Catherine was just too demanding and always looking for things to reprove for him to be anything more than mostly at ease in her presence, and Caroline? Well, he was never truly at ease around any lady who was attempting to convince him to marry her.

"I think you could be if you tried," Bingley retorted.

Darcy shook his head. "To this point in my life, it has been impossible, and I do not see that changing any time soon."

"Very well," Bingley conceded. "I shall attempt to work on you, but I will not be utterly discouraged if I am not immediately successful. It shall be an offering of thanks for the help you are giving me with the estate."

"I think I would rather not receive your gratitude if it is to be given in such a fashion." Darcy drew his horse to a stop. In the field just beyond the fence, there were three riders – one gentleman and two ladies. "It seems we are in luck," he called to Bingley.

"What do you – Oh! Yes, indeed, we are!" Bingley replied as he noticed the riders.

"Do they have a brother?"

Bingley's face pinched. "I am not entirely certain. I believe I remember something about a cousin or brother or some such thing, but..."

"You were far too focused on the ladies to commit that bit of information to memory."

Bingley smiled sheepishly. "I was."

Darcy shook his head. It was just like his friend to put all other thoughts out of his head when discussion of a pretty lady was broached. It would be good for the man to marry if only so he could focus on what needed to be done instead of where a wife might be found. Maybe they would be fortunate, and they would find a steady and calm lady amongst the beauties of Longbourn. Then, Darcy could encourage a courtship while still retaining enough of Bingley's attention to guide him in setting himself up as master of his own domain.

"Shall we approach them?" Darcy asked.

Bingley drew to a halt and looked at his friend with concern. "You wish to meet strangers?"

"For you, I do."

"Not for yourself?" Bingley teased.

Darcy shook his head. "No, I am not eager to marry, but I know you are." He clucked to his horse as he turned him in the direction in which the fence ran. They would approach it slowly and at an angle so as not to look too eager. "You do realize that choosing one lady as a wife will mean not choosing every other lady, no matter how beautiful."

"Yes," Bingley answered tersely. "If you think so meanly of me, I am surprised you would think to offer your sister to me."

"I do not think meanly of you. I merely wished to judge your enthusiasm for marriage. You truly wish to marry? You are only four and twenty."

"And you are eight and twenty. I see no reason why my age should be a detriment to marrying if yours is not one to remaining unmarried. Yes, I know there are not many in our circles who wish to be married so young, but I have my inheritance, and I wish to settle into it as my father desired.

Therefore, it would be best for me to take a wife, so that I can send Caroline to live with Hurst, and my wife can be hostess for you and my other guests."

"So you wish to marry to be rid of Caroline?" Darcy asked with a laugh.

"I do. You should consider it. If you were married, she could not fawn over you as she does now."

Darcy continued to laugh. "That is a worthy argument. I shall have to consider it if I ever find a lady who is to my liking."

"I would not be as fastidious as you for a kingdom!" Bingley declared. "Perfection is rarely found in human form." He smirked. "Except, of course, in the form of the great and noble Fitzwilliam Darcy."

Darcy's eyes narrowed. "I do not think of myself as perfect."

"No, but you do wear an air of superiority at times that suggests you do."

"I do not."

"You do."

"Pick a marker."

"The stile."

"It shall not be as satisfying as thrashing you at Gentleman Jacksons, but..." Darcy did not finish his sentence, opting instead to urge his horse into a gallop. It was a trick he had learned from his cousin, Richard, and had found particularly useful in beating Bingley in a race. The man was not only an expert at making friends, but he was also very good at selecting fast horses.

"It was not a fair race," Bingley grumbled as he reached the stile just behind Darcy.

"No, it was not, but it was excessively satisfying," Darcy replied with a wide grin.

"That was some show of horsemanship," the gentleman in the adjoining field called out.

Bingley doffed his hat and made a grand bow. "My thanks to you, sir."

"Mr. William Bennet," the man said as he approached Darcy and Bingley.

He was a large man, both in height and breadth, with a friendly countenance.

"Mr. Charles Bingley and my friend Mr. Fitzwilliam Darcy." Bingley motioned first to himself and then Darcy.

"Two of my sisters," William said as he motioned for the ladies with him to come forward. "Jane is the eldest and Elizabeth the next after her."

Darcy caught his breath. Uncle or no, Bingley's solicitor was not lying about the beauty of the ladies at Longbourn. Miss Bennet was the sort of lady the masters sought, which made Miss Elizabeth's beauty seem to pale in comparison but not to him. There was something enchanting about the set of her eyes and the slight disproportion of her features. It was *her* beauty, not that of her sister, which had caused his breath to hitch.

He touched his hat and gave a nod in greeting but said nothing. He could not. His tongue seemed to be stone. Thankfully, Bingley's tongue was as loose as ever.

"We were just inspecting this side of the property since a ride after being confined in a carriage seemed to be a most refreshing activity." He looked at Darcy and tipped his head toward the Bennets.

"Indeed, it is," Darcy managed to say.

"Elizabeth loves to ride nearly as much as she enjoys walking," William said. "Jane prefers riding, and I could not choose one over the other even if forced."

"Do you ride here often?" Bingley directed his question to Miss Bennet.

Darcy breathed a sigh of relief, strangely happy that Bingley had not selected Miss Elizabeth.

"Is something amiss, Mr. Darcy?" Elizabeth asked.

Darcy's eyes grew wide, and he shook his head. "No, why do you ask?"

"You were frowning."

"Was I?"

"You are doing it again."

"I am?"

Next to Darcy, Bingley chuckled. "You will have to excuse my friend. He often looks displeased when he is contemplating something. I assure you he is far more pleasant than he appears and often more civil than he sounds."

Darcy scowled at Bingley.

"That," Bingley said triumphantly, "is a truly displeased expression."

Darcy opened his mouth to hand Bingley a retort he well-deserved, but Elizabeth's laughter stopped him and caused his lips to curl in pleasure.

"I thank you for the demonstration, Mr. Bingley," Elizabeth said. "I shall now know the difference between when Mr. Darcy is pensive and when he is vexed."

Bingley, gallant, *helpful* friend that he was, nodded his acceptance of Elizabeth's thanks.

"If you spend enough time with us," Darcy said, arching a brow at his friend, "I am certain you will have ample practice distinguishing the two expressions since Bingley seems to enjoy vexing me. He is such a trying fellow. You have no idea how he tries one's nerves."

"I do not," Bingley retorted.

"Our mother says the same thing about our father," William interrupted.

"Our father intends to call on you tomorrow," Jane inserted.

"I shall look forward to his arrival," Bingley replied. "We do not wish to take you from your ride."

Darcy did not believe a word of it. Bingley looked absolutely smitten and in no rush to leave Miss Bennet.

"You are not," that lady replied with a small duck of her head. "We were only going to ride a bit further and then turn back. This respite has been quite pleasant."

"Indeed, it has been," Bingley replied with one of his charming smiles that he used when speaking to any particularly pretty young woman who had captured his fancy.

"Do you ride here often?" Darcy repeated Bingley's question from before, which had not yet been answered.

"Not so often as I wish," Jane replied. "However, we do take frequent walks along the path to the knoll. The aspect is quite lovely from there. William was thinking of building a bench under the oak tree, as it is Lizzy's favourite place to hide away with a book."

"Perhaps one day you can show me the aspect," Bingley offered. "However, I am not a great reader, so I shall not be carrying a book, although Darcy may bring one with him. And he is often looking for a quiet spot to read. I am afraid I am not overly good at providing such, and my sisters are even worse."

Darcy grimaced. "Indeed," he said dryly.

William laughed. "Sisters can be trying."

"Almost as much as brothers," Elizabeth retorted.

"Ah, but there is only one of me and five of you." William turned to Bingley and Darcy. "While they can be trying, I would not trade them for the world, for they are all delightful in their own way."

Darcy could hear the edge of a warning in the

man's voice. Not one of the Bennet ladies would be left unprotected. Mr. William Bennet would see to that. It was a sentiment that Darcy could both sympathize with and respect. "I feel the same way about my sister."

He held William's gaze for a moment, earning himself a small nod of the man's head.

"We should return home and allow you to continue your inspection." William touched his hat. "Until tomorrow."

Darcy watched as the Bennets rode across the field.

"Miss Bennet is an angel," Bingley said.

"I would agree," Darcy replied as he nudged his horse forward. And her sister was a temptress, he thought, as he cast one more look at the retreating forms of the Bennets. He would be pleased to meet her father and explore her connections more fully. He shook his head. That was not a thought he had ever expected to have. However, if her connections were sound... Well, it might just be possible that he and Bingley could indeed be brothers.

Chapter 5

"How was your ride?" Mr. Bennet asked that evening as the family sat down for dinner. "Mary said you rode in the direction of Netherfield." The right corner of his mouth was lifted in a small smirk, and there was a laugh lying just below his words.

"It was most interesting," Elizabeth replied. "Did you know that if you look at the knoll from a distance with your eyes squinched shut just so," she demonstrated the action, "the trees look almost as if they are made up of daubs and streaks of paints? I am certain even I could replicate it with little effort." She knew precisely what her father was asking, but, seeing as he seemed in a playful sort of mood, she thought to oblige him with a delectable piece of ridiculousness.

Her father chuckled as he passed William a bowl

covered with a cloth. "And will you make an attempt?"

"I should say not!" her mother replied. "And you will not make that expression again, Elizabeth. You shall have lines and wrinkles before you are thirty if you continue to do so."

Elizabeth shared an amused look with her father. "Yes, Mama," she replied.

"Were the trees on the knoll all you saw?" her father asked.

"No, we met Mr. Bingley," Elizabeth replied, adding, "and his friend," over the squeal of delight from her mother.

"Was he handsome? Did he look rich?" Her mother clapped her hands. "Did he take notice of our Jane? She really is too beautiful to be poor."

"None of our daughters will be poor," Mr. Bennet assured her.

"Oh, what do you know of it?" Mrs. Bennet argued. "You rarely attend an assembly. There are so few men of acceptable means. What we need are what Mr. Bingley and his friend provide – wealthy men in want of a wife."

"I do believe that nearly all men are at one point or another in want of a wife whether they be wealthy or no." Mr. Bennet placed a thick piece of beef on his plate. "And what is acceptable to you and what is truly acceptable as far as fortune is concerned are not one and the same."

He smiled at his wife when she gasped at his words. "However, I will agree that our daughters are deserving of the richest men in the kingdom." He held up a finger. "But only if those men are as honorable as they are rich. No daughter of mine shall be given to someone with a healthy bank account but no heart. Nor shall I see them tied to a fool. Those, my lady, are my qualifications for any suitor for *any* of our daughters. No matter how dashing a gentleman might look in a uniform or what carriage he drives."

"But there are so few gentlemen from which to choose," Mrs. Bennet protested. "If we were to travel to Bath, we might do better."

"I dare say we would only find gouty men to marry there," Mary muttered.

"Oh, no!" her mother said with some force. "I have heard tell of many a handsome young man looking for a wife in the Assembly Rooms. Why just last week, Mrs. Goulding was telling me about some fellow who was desperate to marry, so that he could claim his inheritance," she put down her fork and knife and leaned toward the center of the table, "and I can tell you, his inheritance was substantial. Sub-stan-tial." She pronounced each syllable slowly and emphasised it with first a raised brow, then a pointed look, and finally, a vigorous nod of her head.

"As great as Mr. Bingley's?" Their father asked, turning the conversation back to what Elizabeth knew he wished to know.

"Why, yes, if what my sister says is true. Mrs. Goulding told her that this gentleman had nearly six a year. Six! Can you imagine? What fine clothes his wife must have!"

"He has no wife," her father replied. "You said so just a moment ago. Therefore, his wife does not have fine clothes."

Mrs. Bennet huffed in exasperation. "If he had a wife, her clothes would be very fine. Simply the best. They must be, you know, if she is to represent her husband as she ought."

"Did Mr. Bingley have fine clothes?" Mr. Bennet asked Elizabeth.

"He did. He was wearing a blue coat and black

breeches with a hat to match. He looked very dapper. Would you not agree, Jane?"

Jane smiled down at her plate. "Indeed, I would."

"And he seemed to forget the rest of us were even there when he talked to Jane," Elizabeth added. "I dare say he is smitten."

"He is not," Jane refuted weakly.

"What think you, William?" her father asked around the food in his mouth. "Was Mr. Bingley smitten with our Jane, or is Elizabeth seeing only what she wishes to see?"

Elizabeth's eyes narrowed, and she shook her head. Her father enjoyed teasing her about how she liked to assess the character of strangers.

The clink and scratch of cutlery on plates ruled in the room while William swallowed his mouthful of food and washed it down with a sip of wine.

"Elizabeth might be correct. He did seem to single Jane out during our short conversation."

"Oh, I cannot believe you were so fortunate to meet him and on his first day!" Mrs. Bennet cried. "Lady Lucas was certain she would beat me to it and have Charlotte married first. Charlotte is a sweet girl, but she is no Jane." Mrs. Bennet beamed at her eldest daughter before taking a sip of her wine. "Although Charlotte may do very well for you, William."

Elizabeth bit back a giggle and shook her head as William leveled a glare at her instead of their mother.

"Yes, yes, there are few who can compare to Jane," Mr. Bennet said. "However, I should like to know what you thought of the man, William. Do I need to bother calling? Or will he do?"

Elizabeth pulled her lip between her teeth. She was excited for Jane. Mr. Bingley seemed just the sort of gentleman that would love Jane as she deserved. She held her breath for a moment, anxious to have William share his approval but seeing a look of question pass across his face. The expression caused her to remember Mr. Bingley's friend. Mr. Darcy was handsome, if a bit grave, but more than those things he was intriguing. He seemed to always be thinking as they were speaking. His thoughts would shadow his features, pulling at his brow, playing at his mouth, and then relaxing into indifference as whatever it was had been seemingly tucked away for the moment. It was very like what William was doing right now, although William was not so good at feigning indifference.

"It was a good first encounter," William said at last, "but I should be sorry to form an opinion on such a short acquaintance. If Mr. Bingley is as he appears, then, yes, he should do quite well for Jane if she will have him."

"Or if he will have her," Mary muttered.

"And why would he not have her?" Lydia asked. "Jane is the most beautiful of us all. She is even prettier than I am, though she is not taller." She lifted her chin and looked down her nose at Mary.

"I am only saying that a gentleman should be consulted as to his opinion on the matter of his marriage before his future lot is cast in the die," Mary replied. "We are speaking as if the whole of his life has been decided since Jane and Lizzy find him handsome, and he is capable of speaking to them. I just think it unwise to assume the end before the beginning."

"Mary! I do not know where you get these ideas." Mrs. Bennet shook her head. "Of course, he will want Jane. Every gentleman prefers a pretty wife to a plain one." She looked at her daughters one by one. "And none of you are to look as pretty as Jane until we have secured him." She shook her head at Lydia when she opened her mouth to speak. "I know it will be very hard for you, Lydia, but they shall do the same for you when it is your turn."

"They shall all be married before that," Mary muttered, earning her a glare from her youngest sister and a giggle from Kitty.

"If we might return to some sort of sense," Mr. Bennet said. "I am not assuming Mr. Bingley will wish to marry my Jane, though I will find him immensely daft if he does not. I am only asking if he is a good prospect, and William has said that he might be. We shall call on him tomorrow, and then, I will add my voice to William's assessment."

"He seemed very amiable," Jane said softly as her cheeks glowed rosy.

"I shall remember that," her father replied with a wink and a smile. "I shall leave the house with the intention that I will like the man. Then, he has only to lose my good opinion rather than gain it. Will that be to your satisfaction, my dear?"

"Yes, Papa," Jane answered.

"What of his friend?" Mr. Bennet asked, looking at Elizabeth. "Am I supposed to be predisposed to like him as well?"

"I would prefer for you to make your own assessment," Elizabeth replied, though she did hope her father would find Mr. Darcy acceptable.

"You did not find him to your liking, then?"

"I did not say," Elizabeth replied. "You do not intend to meet him until tomorrow, so I do not wish to spoil your enjoyment."

"The impertinence!" her mother cried. "You shall never snare him with such saucy responses." She looked at her younger daughters. "Perhaps Kitty would be better?"

"No," William said sharply, causing everyone to turn their eyes toward him. He slowly put his knife down and took a roll from the covered bowl in front of him. "I mean to say, if Mr. Darcy is worthy of any of my sisters, then it will be Lizzy. He is a serious-looking sort of fellow."

"He has a nicer carriage than Mr. Bingley, who has four thousand a year!" Mrs. Bennet declared. "I do not see how he cannot be worthy of Lizzy."

Elizabeth watched William finger his knife rather than picking it up to put butter on his roll. His eyes were looking at nothing and everything. There was something he was not saying and did not wish to say.

"I was merely thinking of his character as Father

said earlier. We must discover if these gentlemen will treat Jane and Lizzy as they deserve to be treated. I have seen many wealthy gents who showers his wife with money and clothes but neither affection nor respect."

"Oh, I have read stories of such in the paper," Lydia agreed. "What is his name? Kitty and I will look tonight."

Elizabeth wondered from Lydia's tone if her sister would be more pleased to find a tawdry story about Mr. Darcy than to not find one at all. Lydia loved a good story.

"Fitzwilliam Darcy," William replied. "I would not be at all surprised if he is mentioned somewhere in the society pages. His uncle is the Earl of Matlock, after all."

Elizabeth's eyes grew wide, and her mother looked as if she was about to faint away.

"An earl!" Mrs. Bennet exclaimed.

"Yes," William replied. "And men with as much money and connections such as Mr. Darcy has are rarely not in the society pages."

"How much does he have?" Mrs. Bennet asked.

"I have heard ten thousand a year."

Mrs. Bennet fell back in her chair and fanned

herself with her handkerchief. "Ten thousand and an earl!"

"Yes," William muttered. "Which is why we need to proceed cautiously. Men of his standing are not always honorable."

He did not lift his eyes from the roll he was breaking into bits on his plate but not eating. There was definitely something he knew about Mr. Darcy that he was not saying. Elizabeth would not press him on it now, but later. She smiled to herself. Later, she would extract the truth from him.

Chapter 6

Darcy picked at his sleeves, righting every supposed imperfection, while he stood at the window in the drawing room at Netherfield. He glanced at the clock in the corner. It was two minutes past the acceptable time for callers. Hopefully, Mr. Bennet would not be too late in calling. He wished for this interview to be over. His mind had played with the possibilities of how it could go several times last night and then again this morning.

"You seem anxious, Mr. Darcy." Caroline said as she came to stand next to him.

Darcy stepped one step away from her. She always insisted on standing closer to him than what he was comfortable with. However, she was right. He was anxious, and it was not her close proximity which was creating the anxiety. The source of his unease was another lady. He had spent a great deal of time pondering Miss Elizabeth Bennet last night. There was something about the animation of her features when she spoke that would not let him put her out of his mind. Her beauty, he was confident, he could eventually talk himself out of needing to admire, but her spirit was something that captivated him. He felt a deep, unsettling need to see her again. However, he was not going to tell Caroline such. Instead, he merely said what was likely obvious.

"I am just restless."

"We could take a turn of the garden," Caroline suggested. "Louisa would be happy to join us."

Darcy shook his head. "No, I will stay with your brother. He is expecting callers, and I wish to meet them."

Her brows rose. "Indeed?"

He could well understand the skepticism in her voice. He was not known for his enjoyment of meeting new people.

"There cannot be anyone worth meeting," Caroline continued in a tone much sweeter than her words. "It is the country, and a dreadful looking one at that."

"There is more to judging an area than the number of hat shops on the high street."

Darcy smiled. He couldn't help it. Bingley rarely used that tone of censure with his sister.

"Your brother is correct," Darcy added. "Meeting the prominent gentlemen in the area is an important part of the evaluation process."

"And one should do it with a proper attitude," Bingley added, still using his stern voice.

"You are not seriously thinking of remaining here long, are you?" Caroline asked.

"I signed papers for a year," Bingley replied. "I will be staying; whether you do or not is completely up to you. I shall house you as long as you can tolerate it, but an establishment can be set up for you if Hurst will not take you."

Caroline gasped. Her displeasure with being in Hertfordshire had grown last evening upon hearing her brother's effusive praise of Miss Bennet. Today, she seemed determined to sway her brother's opinion through Darcy. However, Darcy was not planning to be a willing party to her scheme.

"It is best to see the area in all seasons," Darcy agreed.

"You cannot mean to stay here as well?" Caroline cried.

Darcy shook head. "I am sure I will need to return to town for my sister, and eventually, I will need to make a journey to Pemberley. However, I will attempt to see this place for at least a portion of time during each of the seasons." And, if at all possible, he would spend a great deal of time in the area so that he could see Miss Elizabeth if her family proved to be acceptable, which brought him back to his current anxiety. He hoped with all that was within him that her father and brother were gentlemen with whom he might form a friendship.

"Are you well?" Caroline asked him.

He startled from his contemplations. "Why do you ask?"

"Your face fell just then as if something was troubling you."

"I was just thinking about all that I have to do," he prevaricated. It was not that at all. If he were to answer her honestly, he would have to admit that his desires as they pertained to Miss Elizabeth and her family were startling to him each time they overtook him – which had been many times since that meeting yesterday.

"We could invite Georgiana to join us," Caroline cooed. "That would surely give your mind some ease, and Louisa and I, some acceptable companionship."

"I am of half a mind to send you back to London on the first coach I find," Bingley snapped. "You know I do not wish to marry Georgiana any more than Darcy wishes to marry you."

Caroline sucked in a sharp breath at his words.

"Oh, do not look at me so," Bingley continued. "Darcy knows full-well that you have set your cap at him, and yet he has not made a move to secure your affections."

"Charles," Louisa scolded. "You are too harsh."

Bingley turned toward his older sister. "She," he pointed at Caroline, "will not give this area or my decision an ounce of respect. She is set against it and determined to colour the whole experience with her displeasure. She has not even met Miss Bennet, with whom she might be able to form a friendship, yet she has dismissed the notion. I am not too harsh."

"You are a trifle sharp," Darcy interjected.

Bingley whirled to face him.

"I am not saying that what you said was incorrect. I have no desire to marry your sister. However, it might not have been said at the most appropriate time." He gave Caroline a small smile. "You are a beautiful, accomplished young woman. There is no deficit in you that causes me to reject you." He sighed. "I just do not believe we would suit, and..."

He shifted uneasily. He did not reveal much of his inner thoughts aloud very often, and when he did, it was never to Caroline Bingley. He sometimes shared them with Bingley and Richard, but beyond that, even his sister was not privy to many of his closely guarded views.

"I wish to marry for love." There he had said it. "I do not love you. Not in that way, at least. You are a friend and the sister of a friend, but, I apologize if this is too blunt, that is all. And no, I do not see that changing."

He placed a hand on her arm as he saw the tears gathering in her eyes. "Believe me, there is no deficiency in you. My affections are just not engaged."

She lifted her chin. "I understand." She turned to her brother. "I will return to greet your guests, but I find I must get some air. Louisa!"

Mrs. Hurst rose quickly from her spot on the

sofa near her husband and escorted her sister out of the room.

"I shall be returning to London before the season," Hurst said from behind the paper he was reading. "I shall take Caroline with me." He lowered the paper for a moment and looked at Darcy. "That was well done, sir. Neither she nor her sister has listened one jot to my opinion on the subject of her being the mistress of Pemberley. They shall have to give it some credence now."

Darcy sighed. He had known that at some point he might have to dash Caroline's hopes, but he had hoped that some other gentleman would catch her fancy and the issue would take care of itself.

"You wish to marry for love," Bingley said with a grin.

Darcy nodded. "As you know. However, I do apologize for causing your sister pain."

"She is the cause of her own pain," Bingley retorted. "I just hope she can accept your words and begin to look for a husband in earnest."

"I doubt she is completely daft," Darcy replied.

"You'd be surprised," Hurst muttered from behind his paper, causing Bingley to laugh and Darcy to shake his head and grin.

~*~*~

"Mr. Bennet, Mr. William Bennet," Bingley rose from his seat and greeted the gentlemen as they entered the drawing room half an hour later.

Darcy had finally relaxed enough to sit in a chair and participate in a discussion about the fields they had seen on their morning ride. Now, however, as the gentlemen he had eagerly anticipated entered the room, his nerves once again rose to an uncomfortable pitch. He tugged his sleeves straight and fidgeted with the buttons on his waistcoat. At this moment, he would very much like to take Caroline up on her offer to walk around the garden. He doubted, though, that Mr. Bennet and his son would be disposed to accepting such a suggestion, and Bingley, no doubt, would be equally as unwilling a participant since the tea he had ordered was just being brought into the room. Therefore, Darcy would take his seat and endure the discomfort of remaining motionless. He was certain that it would have been better to meet these gentlemen in the field with a gun, a few dogs, and the chance of securing a pheasant dinner. Calls in the drawing rooms were, in his opinion, made the best use of by gentlemen when courting lady.

"I understand my eldest daughters came upon you while riding yesterday," Mr. Bennet said as soon as he settled onto a settee. "I believe William made all the proper introductions."

"Indeed, he did," Bingley assured him. "It was a delightful surprise to meet some of my new neighbours so soon upon my arrival."

Though Darcy's eyes were on Mr. Bennet, he could also see that William Bennet was studying him carefully. He shifted his eyes to the young man and made note of the small scowl he wore.

"Have you spent much time in the country?" Mr. Bennet was asking Bingley when Darcy turned his attention back to the conversation.

"I have spent a considerable amount of time at Pemberley, but this is the first time that I will be officially residing somewhere other than in a town. My father's business was in manufacturing, so we lived in Manchester. In fact, his sister and her husband are still there."

"My brother Gardiner is in trade," Mr. Bennet answered with a smile. "He does right well, I can tell you that. He has as fine a home as can be found near Cheapside and warehouses that are never idle."

Darcy tipped his head to the side, and one eyebrow rose as he contemplated how his relations might react to such ties should he decide to pursue Miss Elizabeth. Lady Catherine would never be satisfied with any choice he made that was not of her own choosing, but Lord Matlock? Well, there were political advantages to having some connections in trade. "What sort of things does he store in his warehouses?"

"Mainly textiles, although he is not opposed to accepting a shipment of spices, tea, or any other good with a healthy profit margin." The right side of Mr. Bennet's mouth tipped up, and a sparkle, not unlike the one Darcy had seen in Elizabeth's eyes, settled into her father's eyes. "Gardiner inherited most of the intelligence in his family."

"Indeed?" Darcy's brows rose.

"He is the most sensible one of the three. Did you meet Mrs. Philips?" Mr. Bennet asked Bingley.

He nodded.

"She is nice but a bit flighty, is she not?"

Bingley shrugged. "I really could not say."

Mr. Bennet laughed. "Very well, I will not force you to be impolite. I shall take on that task myself. I can tell you, having been married to her sister for these past twenty-three years, that Mrs. Philips is indeed flighty and as good at carrying a tale as the society papers in the *Times*. My wife is very similar. Gardiner, however, cares not one jot for gossip that cannot benefit his business and has a head for numbers that is matched by few. I assure you he is the most sensible of the three."

"He sounds an interesting sort of chap," Bingley commented.

"That he is. My eldest daughters are favourites of him and his wife, while my youngest are favourites of Mrs. Philips. I know of what I speak when comparing sensibilities."

Darcy was not altogether sure he enjoyed hearing a gentleman speak so of his family on so short an acquaintance.

"It is best if you know the particulars before you are subjected to my wife's schemes."

Ah. That made sense.

"Is she a matchmaker?" Darcy asked.

"Only if a gentleman meets her qualifications," Mr. Bennet said with a chuckle, "and if her sister's intelligence is accurate, I believe both of you have enough qualifications to your names to be worthy of her daughters."

A fortune hunter? Darcy had met enough of those in his seasons.

"Do not look so frightened, Mr. Darcy. I assure you, you will not be trapped in some unscrupulous scheme. Mrs. Bennet's daughters are to be prized, which is something on which I do not disagree with my wife. But unlike my wife, whose main goal is to see her daughters well-settled without a worry for their financial care – and who can blame a mother for wishing such for her children – my desires for them extend to their emotional well being."

"My sisters will not marry without love and respect," William inserted with a curiously pointed look for Darcy. He had seemed a very pleasant sort of fellow yesterday. Darcy was uncertain what had transpired between then and now to cause him to be so skeptical.

"I wish the same for my sister," Darcy replied. "My cousin, Colonel Fitzwilliam, and I are her guardians now that my parents are no longer with us," he added.

"How old is she?" William asked.

"Not yet sixteen."

"The same age as my Lydia," Mr. Bennet said.

"It can be a trying age. I should know since I have endured it four times already. I wish you well with your task, sir."

"Thank you. I hope to succeed with it."

Mr. Bennet tipped his head. "You sound unsure of yourself."

"I have had a setback as of late," Darcy replied.

"I hope it was nothing too serious."

Darcy blew out a breath. "The trouble was discovered in time."

"Does she travel with you?" William asked.

Darcy shook his head. "My aunt thought it best for her to remain in town and continue her lessons."

"Lady Matlock?"

"You know of my connections?" Darcy replied to William. The fact that William knew Darcy was related to Lord Matlock and still looked at him with suspicion rather than just promoting his sister spoke well of the man to Darcy. It seemed William was adamantly truthful about his sisters not marrying for anything other than love and respect.

"Several of them," William replied.

There was a lifting of one brow that accompanied a pointed look which spoke of the young man knowing something that Darcy should realize was not a recommendation of his character.

"I should be interested to hear all you know at some point." Darcy rose as Caroline and Louisa entered the room with Hurst and were introduced. He chuckled to himself as he realized he would no longer be the object of the younger Bennet's scrutiny. Caroline would have that pleasure.

"We do not wish to overstay our welcome," Mr. Bennet said after a few minutes of small talk with the ladies. "I will extend an invitation to you all to call on us at Longbourn, but I will do it with the warning that my wife will attempt to discover your favorite dishes and will insist that you join us for dinner."

Again, the right corner of his mouth tipped up, and his eyes twinkled. "She wished for me to make the invitation myself, but she will get far more pleasure extending it to you herself, so I refused her pleas. I will, however, inform you that she is the best hostess in the area, and our cook is excellent. You will not be disappointed, should you choose to accept her offer."

He handed his teacup to Bingley and pushed up

from the settee. "William and I will look forward to seeing you in the future as well. In fact, William will be riding out tomorrow morning. I suspect you are the sort who enjoys an early morning ride as much as he does."

"Indeed, we do," Bingley agreed eagerly.

"He will be riding alone," Mr. Bennet cautioned with a grin.

"As will we," Bingley replied, "although if I am with Darcy, and he is with me, we are not truly alone, are we?"

Mr. Bennet joined Bingley in a hearty laugh.

He took his hat from the butler. "It has been a joy to meet you, and I do not say that to most. In fact, if I were to be honest, I try my best to avoid meeting new people – old ones, too." He winked. "I prefer books."

He gave his farewells to the Hursts and Caroline and was gone, William following closely behind him.

Darcy looked at the clock. Fifteen minutes almost to the second. It was possible that he might be able to like Mr. Bennet. The man was short on calls and, according to his own account, a lover of books. He released a sigh. Now, if only he could fig-

ure out what it was that the younger Bennet held
against him.

Chapter 7

Placing her bonnet on the table near the door and beginning to unfasten her pelisse upon returning from her walk the next day, Elizabeth smiled as she saw Jane descending the stairs. For once, she would not have to break her fast alone.

"Did you see William?" Jane asked eagerly.

Elizabeth chuckled. "No. Nor did I see Mr. Bingley or Mr. Darcy."

Jane sighed. "Do you think they will call on us? Papa told them they may."

"I was there," Elizabeth reminded her sister.

Their poor father had been thoroughly questioned by their mother about the house, both Mr. Bingley's and Mr. Darcy's clothes, the demeanor of both gentlemen, and the type of china in which the tea was served, as well as about Mr. Bingley's other guests. Mr. Bennet had borne it as patiently as a gentleman might until he had answered each question twice. Upon the third presentation of a question regarding if the butler seemed pleased to be serving his new master, Mr. Bennet told his wife that she might gather all the information she needed the following day as he was certain that Mr. Bingley would be calling on Longbourn since Mr. Bennet had given him leave to do so.

"But are you not eager to see them again?" Jane wrapped an arm around Elizabeth's and went with her to the breakfast room.

"Perhaps not so eager as you," Elizabeth teased.

"Is he not perfect? His features are so animated when he speaks, and his hair is just the most divine mix of sunshine and sunset."

"Jane!" Elizabeth said with a laugh. "You sound more like Lydia than yourself."

Jane sighed as she took her seat. "He is just so handsome and amiable."

Elizabeth could not deny that. Mr. Bingley appeared to be all that a young man should be – handsome, pleasant, and rich. She smiled. Even she sounded a bit like her youngest sister.

"Good morning, Papa," she said as her father entered to gather his cup of tea and a plate of toast and jam before burying himself in his book room for a morning of reading in relative silence.

"Good morning, Lizzy, Jane." He poured his tea into his cup and looked up at Jane with a smirk. "Has William returned from his ride?"

"No, and Elizabeth did not see him," Jane replied in a very sincere and concerned tone.

Mr. Bennet drew out his watch, looked at it, glanced at the clock on the mantle, and with a shrug, returned the watch to his pocket. "It is only early yet. However, when he does return, I wish to speak with him first."

Jane pulled a lip between her teeth and nodded while her father chuckled.

"I shall not keep him long. I only wish to know something about a field." He placed a second piece of toast, smeared with jam, on his plate and prepared to exit the room. "I would expect him in no more than an hour. I know how he likes to eat his breakfast before the sun is too high in the sky."

An hour later, Jane paced from the window to her seat in the sitting room, sat for a moment, and then paced back to the window. "It has been an hour," she said to Elizabeth. "He should be here by now."

"He is likely just enjoying himself. He does not have other gentlemen to ride with every day," Elizabeth replied.

"Oh, but he will be hungry," Mrs. Bennet added. "I always tell him to take an apple or a biscuit with him, but he refuses. And now he shall faint of hunger, and Longbourn will be without an heir. I am certain I could never be at ease seeing Longbourn given to some stranger."

"Mama, he shall not perish from hunger after one day," Elizabeth said.

"One never knows," Mrs. Bennet argued. "He will be weak, and if he should perchance get his feet wet, he will not be strong enough to fight off the illness that will arise and then after an excruciating period of fever during which we shall attempt to make him at ease — but it will be impossible — he shall gasp his last and leave us to another."

"Mama!" Elizabeth cried.

"We could go look for him," Jane sat on the edge of her chair, looking excessively excited. "We could take an apple with us."

Mrs. Bennet's hand flew to her heart. "Oh, you are so good, Jane." She turned to Elizabeth. "Why did you not think of that?"

"Because I do not believe William is in any grave danger. He is only a few minutes later than expected."

Mrs. Bennet pursed her lips and shook her head. "Go with your sister. I cannot have both William and Jane missing. Surely if you are with her, there is little chance that anything ill will befall her."

"Do you not care if Lizzy does not return?" Mary asked.

"Whatever would possess you to ask such a thing?" her mother demanded. "Of course, I shall be devastated if Elizabeth does not return, but one must realize that of all my daughters, Jane is the most beautiful and likely the one to ensure that if something happens to William, I and any remaining unwed children, of which you may be one, will be well-cared-for should the worst befall your father."

Elizabeth was not certain if she should be insulted by her mother words or simply pleased that, should she not return, she would be missed. She did not stay in the room long enough to hear the argument that was about to erupt between Mary and their mother. Mama would likely be calling for her salts soon enough as she would talk herself into flutters. Instead, Elizabeth hurried up to her room behind Jane and prepared to set out to find her missing brother.

~*~*~

"When you marry Mr. Bingley," Elizabeth began when she and Jane had ridden far enough from the stables to not be heard by anyone, "you shall have to invite Mary to visit you in town. I am certain Mr. Bingley will not always remain at Netherfield, and if we do not wish to have Papa driven to an early grave due to the incessant arguing between Mama and Mary, we must see Mary well-matched soon."

Jane giggled. "They have been bickering a great deal lately."

"I think it is the way Mama critiques everything Mary does. It is always wanting in some way. She is not so lively as Lydia, she is not so accomplished as Mama expects her to be, and she is not so beautiful as you – not that any of us is."

Jane gasped.

"You know it is true, Jane. Not one of us can compare to you in beauty. Although Lydia does come close, she does not have your sweet spirit."

Jane shook her head. "Kitty. Kitty is far prettier than I am."

"Kitty?" Elizabeth's voice was filled with incredulity.

"Yes, Kitty." Jane replied. "When she is not following Lydia's advice and just dresses herself as she wishes, she is pretty, and in a year or two she will be the one all the young men will be seeking." Jane smiled broadly at Elizabeth. "That should make Lydia excessively perturbed!"

"Our poor father!" Elizabeth cried as both she and Jane dissolved into laughter for a moment. They both knew that Lydia expected to be the one to step into Jane's place when Jane married. It did not matter to Lydia that she was the youngest. She was only second in her mind to Jane.

"Mr. Crenshaw," Jane said when they had sobered.

"What do you mean?"

"I will not have to find a husband for Mary. Mr. Crenshaw has been paying her particular attention at assemblies for the last year, and he always appears to be very happy to see her if we happen to meet him in Meryton."

Elizabeth's brow furrowed as she thought. Mr. Crenshaw had been polite in every meeting, and he had asked both her and Mary as well as Jane to dance. "Are you certain he has singled her out?"

Jane nodded. "Watch him at the next assembly. He will ask us each to dance, but he will not be as animated dancing with us as he will be with Mary. And, if you watch him when he is not dancing, you will see that he is often looking in her direction."

"Truly?"

Jane nodded.

Elizabeth had not paused to notice such things at assemblies. She had been so busy looking for possible matches for Jane that she had not once thought about Mary. She would have to make an effort to be more attentive at the next assembly.

"He is very nice," she said after a moment of silent contemplation.

"And pleasing to the eye," Jane added with a smirk.

"True," Elizabeth agreed. Mr. Crenshaw was not tall and dashing, but he was not short either. And his features reminded her of those that a sculptor might chisel out of marble. He was neither portly nor thin, and she had to admit he always smelled rather nice.

"That, along with the fact that his farm does very

well, will make him a most acceptable choice for Mary. She shall want for nothing." Jane looked at Elizabeth. "And even William approves of him. I asked — last night as I was thinking about the assembly and remembered Mr. Crenshaw." She sighed. "It will be the most perfect assembly ever if Mr. Bingley asks me to dance."

Elizabeth chuckled. "It will be indeed."

"And Mr. Darcy will ask you."

"If William allows it," Elizabeth muttered.

"Whatever do you mean?"

"Have you not noticed how uneasy William seems when he speaks of Mr. Darcy?"

Jane shook her head.

"Well, I have, and I have been determined to ask him about it. However, I still have not had the opportunity to do so. There must be something about Mr. Darcy of which William knows and does not approve. Perhaps I should not even like him."

"But how can you not?" Jane cried. "He is very handsome and rich – very, very rich!"

"Yet, if his character is wanting," Elizabeth refuted. She drew her horse to a stop. "This is the field Papa said William was going to, is it not?"

Jane looked in all directions. "I believe so."

"And yet he is not here."

"Mr. Jones," Jane called to a man who was plucking fruit from a tree in the orchard that stood next to the field in which they rode."

"Aye, miss," the gentleman climbed down from his ladder and came to stand by the stone wall that enclosed the orchard. He wiped his brow with a handkerchief and then replaced his hat. "How might I be of service?"

"Have you seen William?" Jane asked.

"Aye," the man glanced at the sky, "some time ago now. He and I and the two gents with him had a good discussion about the piece of wall in need of repair. Those boards will not hold back the cattle for long, especially after the winter does her work."

"I am certain Father will have it repaired before the trees are flowering in the spring," Jane replied with a smile.

"I do not doubt it, miss. Your father is a good man, but there are only so many hands to complete so much work."

"True, but my father adores jam on his toast – damson jam in particular – so I dare say, you shall be first on his list of things to be seen to."

"A good jam is a pleasure. That's for certain,"

Mr. Jones agreed with a chuckle. "I like it right well myself."

"How is the baby?" Jane asked.

"He's a joy, miss. Fat and pink, he is. He'll be in church this Sunday."

"I am glad to hear it," Jane said.

"As am I," Elizabeth added.

"Those gents will be there as well. The tall one – Mr. Darcy – said he'd be pleased to meet my Zachary. They both seemed very nice sorts of fellows." He removed his hat once again and dried his brow. "They and the young Mr. Bennet were headed toward Oakham Mount, though I think the young Mr. Bennet was talking about only going as far as the wood."

"Thank you, Mr. Jones." Jane dipped her head, an action that was met with a small bow from Mr. Jones before he returned to his work.

"Do you wish to go to the wood first or Oakham Mount?" Elizabeth asked.

"It seems silly to go to Oakham Mount before the wood if William was talking of going there, do you not think?"

Elizabeth nodded, and the two turned toward

the wood that stood between Longbourn and Oakham Mount.

Chapter 8

Darcy turned quickly toward William. "What did you say?"

"That militia is due to arrive in Meryton soon," William replied.

"Who is their colonel?" Normally, the arrival of a regiment in an area caused little concern to Darcy beyond what was standard. The increase in men in an area always came with some inherent tribulations if those men were to be of the rowdy sort, and then there was the ever-present issue of providing accommodations as needed as well as food and supplies. However, this time Darcy had a reason for increased concern.

William shrugged. "Forster, I believe, is what Sir William said when he called last, and if anyone knows the happenings of Meryton better than the gossips, it's Sir William Lucas."

Darcy had heard a rumor that Wickham had attached himself to some militia. He would have to ask his cousin to see if Richard knew under whose command Wickham would be.

"Do you know this Colonel Forster?" William asked.

Darcy shook his head. "But my cousin might."

"The town will be less serene once they arrive," Bingley commented. He stopped and picked up a rock to toss into the stream beside which they were walking. Upon getting to the shade of the woods with its low hanging branches, they had decided that dismounting and leading their horses would be the best way to proceed, and then, William had suggested they water their mounts at this stream.

"As will be Longbourn's sitting room," William muttered.

"Do you provide lodging?" Darcy asked.

William shook his head. "That would be ill-advised considering the number of sisters I have," he replied with a laugh. "The officers will find their way to our house well enough, however." He shook his head again. "And my mother and youngest sisters will welcome them with great delight."

"Ah," Darcy commented. "A gentleman in a

smart red coat can turn a head or two – at least, that is what my cousin says."

"He is most certainly right!" William said.

"Do all of your sisters prefer red coats to other colours?" Bingley asked.

William chuckled. "Not all. Lydia certainly, Kitty most likely, but the others are looking for more than a smart jacket."

Darcy stopped and stood for a moment at the edge of the stream. What a trial it must be to have five sisters for whom to care. He had found his one sister enough of a trial, and Bingley's two sisters were forever giving him trouble. Five! To see all five well-matched and wed!

"I believe one of my sisters was impressed by a blue coat the other day," William added with an amused look for Bingley, who grinned in response.

"It is a fine coat. Cost me a good deal, but it is as long in value as it is in good looks."

"Bingley is as much enamoured with fashion as is his sister. However, he is more frugal," Darcy teased. He was finding it easy to be relaxed the longer they moved through the countryside together.

"And does your sister have any preference for

coats?" William asked, keeping his eyes directed forward, though Darcy noticed the poor fellow's ears growing red.

"Whichever one Darcy might be wearing," Bingley responded with a laugh.

"Is that how it is?" William asked.

"No!" Darcy exclaimed. "That is not how it is." He did not want the brother of the lady he wished to know better to think he already belonged to another.

"It is how Caroline would wish it," Bingley replied.

Darcy glared at Bingley until he caught his eye, then he tipped his head toward William. Had he not been listening last evening when Darcy had been telling him how William Bennet seemed to admire Caroline?

Bingley's eyes grew wide, and he stumbled. "She has no hope of securing Darcy," Bingley added hastily. "His affections lie elsewhere."

"You are betrothed."

Darcy blinked. It was not a question but a statement as if William knew that it was a fact. "No, I am not."

"Not to Miss Bingley," William agreed.

"Not to anyone," Darcy refuted.

"No one?" William asked.

Darcy shook his head. "Why would you think I am?"

William shrugged. "Just a rumour I heard, although the source seemed good enough to be believed."

Fallen leaves crunched under boots and hooves.

"Have you met any of my relations?" Darcy asked. There was a hoped-for betrothal about which only those close to the family would know, but he did not think any of them would speak of it, save, perhaps, for his Aunt Catherine.

"No," William replied.

Darcy's chest constricted as realization dawned on him. There was one other person who might bandy about the supposed betrothal. He looked up through the leaves at the sky. The sun was climbing higher in the clear blue beyond the trees' canopy. "It is growing late."

Bingley pulled out his watch. "It is not so very late." He snapped the timepiece closed and tucked it back into his pocket.

"Late enough," Darcy retorted. "By the time we have returned, I will be far beyond hungry."

Bingley looked at him skeptically as well he should. Darcy always ate something before going for a ride, and he had just indulged in some wild berries. Darcy shook his head and hoped Bingley would not press the issue. If William Bennet was a friend or even an acquaintance of George Wickham, Darcy wanted nothing to do with either William or any member of his family.

"If you insist." Bingley's look of disbelief remained in place. "But we might come across more berries."

"I would rather have a cup of tea and a piece of toast." Far away from any of Wickham's associates. Darcy stepped to turn back in the direction from which they had come. However, his foot found some damp leaves covering a rock and slid off of the rock. His ankle twisted as his foot slipped, and down he went.

"Oh, do not move." A feminine voice called as Darcy attempted to rise.

His right hip, having made contact with the rock when he landed, smarted more than his pride and that combined with the ache in his ankle gave him incentive to not refute the instructions. He cursed his boot, the leaves, and that blasted rock for keeping him from his escape and instead, throwing him in front of the very lady he was hoping to forget once he returned to Netherfield.

William helped first Elizabeth and then Jane from their horses.

"What have you done to poor Mr. Darcy?" Elizabeth teased her brother. "Did he say something not to your liking?"

"It was simply wet leaves," Darcy answered. "I am certain in a moment, as soon as I have recovered my breath, I shall be well and able as ever to return to Netherfield."

"Longbourn is closer," Elizabeth said, as she motioned for William to do something.

Darcy's eyes grew wide as William knelt at his feet and placed his hands on Darcy's ankle.

"I know the boot has likely saved you any serious injury," William said apologetically. "However, if I do not assure my sisters that you are well, one of them will likely take on the task of examining your ankle in my stead." He shot a displeased look at Elizabeth, who pressed her lips together to keep from smiling.

Darcy willingly allowed William to prod and poke his ankle before bending it this way and that.

He did not wish for Miss Elizabeth to conduct such an evaluation. She was distracting enough just standing there.

Darcy blew out a breath when William moved to stand up. "As I said, all is well."

Elizabeth crossed her arms. "Then I should like to see you stand on it."

"Do you not believe I can?" Darcy questioned.

"You nearly hid your discomfort," she answered. "Longbourn is closer," she added.

"I can ride my horse. There is no need to walk, so it makes little difference whether I stop at Longbourn or continue to Netherfield."

"The surgeon can be summoned faster from Longbourn than Netherfield, and the longer you let that foot hang at the side of your horse, the more swollen it will become."

"Are you always so argumentative?" Darcy snapped. His foot was throbbing, and she was correct. He did not know which was worse.

"Only when speaking to someone with little sense," Elizabeth retorted. "Do as you will, but I do hope you do not mind having your boot cut off our foot. It seems a waste to ruin such a nice piece of leather."

"We could remove the boot now," Bingley suggested.

"No!" Darcy growled. "Just help me onto my horse."

"Come, Jane," Elizabeth said. "Give William the apple." She was already mounting her horse with William's help.

It seemed to Darcy that William was always ready to bend to his sister's will, and Miss Elizabeth with the fine eyes? Well, she was nothing more than a harridan in a pretty package. Bingley could call at Longbourn if he wished, but Darcy would not be setting one foot outside of Netherfield, not that he could at present even if he wished to do so. Blasted leaves! He gritted his teeth as he placed his weight on his foot and managed to hoist himself onto his horse.

"We will send someone for the surgeon," Miss Bennet assured Mr. Bingley before following Elizabeth.

"You do not need to see me home," Darcy said to William.

William shook his head. "You almost convinced me."

"I beg your pardon?" Darcy asked.

"I thought perhaps my source was painting you with a cruel brush as you did not appear to be as cold as he described. However, I see I am wrong."

"Your source is a liar," Darcy snapped.

"I had thought so as he did tend to be very good at changing a story to suit the crowd around him, but what kind-hearted gentleman rejects the help of a lady who is thinking only of his wellbeing? He does not. An arrogant one does." He clucked to his horse and rode a distance away before turning and stopping to look back. "I cannot stop you from calling at Longbourn, but I shall not be recommending either of you to my sisters or my father."

"Well done," Bingley grumbled. "And no, I shall not be marrying your sister just because you have ruined my chances with Miss Bennet."

Darcy nudged his horse forward. "I do not want to be examined in the home of a stranger," Darcy called after him. "How is that wrong?"

Bingley said nothing. He just galloped away.

"Blasted leaves," Darcy muttered as he urged his horse to go faster while concentrating on keeping his foot from getting jostled too much.

~*~*~

Darcy leaned back on propped up pillows and

looked around his room – the room in which he would pass many hours over the next day or two. The surgeon had assured him that the ankle was only sprained and with a few days of rest would be well on its way back to full strength.

"Your writing things, sir." Darcy's valet placed a small desk on the bed.

Darcy placed it across his legs and unfolded the slope before sliding the drawer that ran the length of the top open and preparing his pen and ink for writing. Withdrawing a sheet of paper from its drawer, he began his letter to his cousin.

He had half a mind to tell his man to prepare for travel and be gone from here, but his conscience would not allow him to forget his promise to his friend. He blew out an exasperated breath. He also could not drive from his mind the face of Elizabeth Bennet.

He paused in his writing. She had been correct. His foot had swollen a good deal before he had gotten to Netherfield. In fact, he had considered stopping at Longbourn so that he could remove his boot. Thankfully, his valet had been insistent that it could be pulled from his person rather than cut.

It had not been a pleasant extraction, but the boot had been saved.

"Mr. Darcy."

His man was back.

"Miss Bingley is without and would like to know if there is anything you require. She has even volunteered to read to you if needed."

Darcy's brows raised. Bingley must be more than a trifle angry at him, or Caroline would never have made it so far as his door. He shook his head.

"I am certain you can procure whatever might be needed, and as I have not injured my eyes or my head, I am capable of reading to myself."

"I shall tell her, sir."

"I will, however, be in need of having my meals brought up on a tray," he called after his man, and then turned his attention back to his letter. He disliked using only half a sheet, but there was not much to tell his cousin. He had shared that the ladies at Longbourn were as beautiful as they were fabled to be, that he had injured his ankle, that Netherfield seemed a fine, solid house, and that he had reason to believe the younger Mr. Bennet was an associate of Wickham. He followed that assertion with his request for information about which militia Wickham had joined. That was all that was needed. Therefore, whether half a sheet of words or a full sheet written twice over, this paper was going to be folded and sent.

Darcy secured all of his supplies in his desk and moved it to the side of the bed. He would have his man see that letter sent express as soon as possible. With a sigh, he picked up the book he had been reading from the table next to the bed.

"Blasted leaves," he muttered as he prepared to pass a few of the long, lonely hours before him with some poetry.

Chapter 9

Jane glared at Elizabeth from across the sitting room. She had not spoken one word to her since they left the wood. Jane was not one to raise her voice and allow her anger to spill forth in unguarded words when she was put out. No. She usually became a wall of silence – firm and impenetrable until she was prepared to have a discussion with whoever had offended her.

Such silence accompanied by that glare was more than Elizabeth's guilt-ridden heart could withstand. She very much disliked it when Jane was angry with her. She needed to right the wrong that stood between them. However, she knew Jane would not air her grievances in front of their mother and sisters. Therefore, Elizabeth rose from her place and returned her stitching to the basket on the table. "I am going for a walk in the garden." She looked at Jane. "Would you like to join me?"

The eyebrow over Jane's left eye arched.

"Please," Elizabeth said softly.

"She has had too much sun as it is," Mrs. Bennet declared. "We cannot risk her turning brown."

"Please," Elizabeth mouthed.

Jane's eyes narrowed, and her lips pursed before she sighed. "I will wear my wide-brimmed bonnet," Jane assured her mother. "The one I wear to tend the flowers."

"Just the same, stay in the shade as much as possible," their mother called after them. "A gentleman does not want a wife who looks as if she had been put to sea."

Jane took her hat from the hook on the wall near the door at the rear of the house.

"Forgive me," Elizabeth said as soon as their feet had reached the garden path. "I should not have argued."

"No, you should not have," Jane agreed. "When will you learn to hold your tongue?"

Elizabeth sighed. "Not soon enough, I am afraid."

Gaining Jane's forgiveness was only the first step

in setting things to right. Elizabeth knew she also needed to speak to William, whom she had seen circling the garden from the window in the sitting room. While Jane might offer her forgiveness — grudgingly though it currently appeared to be — forgiveness between sisters was not enough to undo the wrong that Elizabeth's propensity to argue had created.

"Let me talk to William. There must be something we can do to fix this mess I have created. Mr. Darcy's response to my insistence was not so very unusual. I am certain any gentleman would have been less than polite when his foot was injured. I should have considered that."

Jane wrapped her arm around Elizabeth's, a sure sign that her anger was fading. "I cannot believe William wishes to cut ties with both Mr. Darcy and Mr. Bingley over a few cross words."

"I do not believe he truly will once he has had time for his anger to cool," Elizabeth said hopefully.

"He is very protective of us," Jane cautioned. "He may not change his mind."

It was a possibility that Elizabeth had considered. William could be stubborn to a fault at times, especially when it came to family and how they should be treated. While it was an endearing trait of his that he cared so much for his sisters, there were moments when it did become a hindrance – such as now.

"Even if he does not change his mind," Elizabeth assured Jane, "I will find a way for you to see Mr. Bingley, even if I have to walk to Netherfield myself and apologize to Mr. Darcy."

"You would do that for me?"

Elizabeth nodded. "I would do just about anything for you, my dear sister, even humiliating myself by begging forgiveness from a gentleman who should be seeking it from me."

Jane laughed lightly. "You are too good."

"I am not, and you know it. That is why our brother is stomping around the garden. Be careful of the rose bushes," she called to William, who was swatting at the trees and bushes with his walking stick as he moved along the path.

"I would not dare harm them," William called back. "And, I am not going to change my mind, Lizzy." He straightened his shoulders and lifted his chin. "No matter how pathetic Jane might attempt to look. Those gentlemen are not the sort that deserve my sisters."

"Everyone spits an angry word at one time or another," Elizabeth replied as they approached him. "And I am very good at provoking such words." She smiled at William.

He sighed and shook his head. "You are a proficient at it, but it is more than that. They are just not the sort of gentlemen with whom I would like to see my sisters."

Oh! He was infuriating at times!

"What is it then?" Elizabeth asked. "You cannot just declare someone unfit to marry without reason. You know I will not just accept your decree without proof."

William scowled at the veracity of such a statement.

"You have not liked Mr. Darcy since you heard his name," Elizabeth continued. "You were cautious about him as if you knew something about him when discussing it with Father at dinner on the day we met them. Yet, Lydia has not found anything unflattering in the papers tied to his name, so what is it that you are not saying?"

William held Elizabeth's gaze for a long, silent,

stubborn minute. "Very well," he finally said. "I have heard that he is not as he appears, but gossip is not right."

"Neither is sending away a perfectly amiable and handsome gentleman, whom I like very much, for no apparent reason," Jane said firmly. "I do not wish to die a beautiful spinster, William – at least, not without knowing why it must be so."

William handed her his handkerchief. "There is no need for tears."

"There is when you are three and twenty and not allowed to marry anyone!" Jane cried with a stamp of her foot – a rare display of temper for her.

William turned away from them, walking three paces forward and then returning. That he did not wish to say anything was evident in his every feature, yet he could not look at Jane dabbing her eyes with his handkerchief without shaking his head and beginning an explanation. "Mr. Darcy was supposed to install his father's godson as the rector of a valuable living. It was written in his father's will. Yet, when the position fell open, Mr. Darcy refused to do as his father had instructed, and now, because Mr. Darcy is an arrogant – " he cleared his throat, "man..."

Elizabeth was certain that was not the word William had wanted to use.

"...there is a man who is having to shift his way through the world when he should be preaching sermons and stirring the fire in the hearth of his parsonage."

"Could there not be a reason for Mr. Darcy's refusal?" Elizabeth asked.

William turned toward her. "This same man told me Mr. Darcy is betrothed, and yet, today, when I asked him, he denied it."

"Perhaps because he is not betrothed," Elizabeth argued. It was very unusual for William to believe one person over another so adamantly. Had he even paused to consider that Mr. Darcy might know more about his being betrothed than someone else? Whatever other bits of information William had heard about Mr. Darcy must be colouring his judgment.

"You are very argumentative, Lizzy Bennet," William spat.

"Only when I am speaking to those who are refusing to use the good sense the Lord gave them!"

"No, not only then. Any time you think you are

right – which is nearly always." William crossed his arms and glared at her.

Elizabeth pulled herself straight. Was there no one who was willing to sort this thing out? How difficult could it be to set things to right? "You will not discover the truth for your sister?" She motioned to Jane.

"I know the truth, and it is that Mr. Darcy is a cold man and any friend of his is not to be trusted."

Elizabeth rolled her eyes and huffed. He only knew what he thought was the truth. Truly, William could be as stubborn and set in his ways as their mother! "One angry exchange? Is that all the evidence you have?"

William did not reply.

"I thought so." She held his gaze. He could glare at her as long as he liked. She would not be driven away by a look of displeasure when she knew she was right, and he needed to reconsider his position.

"I did not say Mr. Bingley could not call," he finally said.

"No, but you will likely sway Papa, and then what does it matter. I shall die an old maid." Jane wiped her eyes once again as she looked upward in an attempt not to let any more tears fall.

"You will not," Elizabeth said, wrapping an arm around Jane's shoulders. "*I* will not allow it to happen."

"And I shall not say a word to Father unless asked," William added. Tears from any of his sisters were his weakness. "At least, I will not say a word about Mr. Bingley that is. I may tell him about Mr. Darcy."

Elizabeth arched a brow.

"He is not what you think he is. I have only told you a portion," William replied.

"And who is this gentleman who has told you these things? Is he a man of high morals? Is his reputation so far beyond reproach that you would risk our sister's happiness?" Elizabeth could not say why she was so determined to hold to the idea that William was wrong about Mr. Darcy. Perhaps it was because Mr. Darcy was handsome, or perhaps it was because his eyes had spoken of sincerity when they had first met. She had seen the way he pondered things before speaking. He was not a gentleman to act brashly. There must be some other explanation for the living not to be bestowed as intended. There just must be.

"Mr. Darcy's actions today confirm the truth of what I have heard," William retorted.

Elizabeth shook her head. Mr. Darcy had spoken crossly, but that did not mean he was always cross or cold. However, she knew that trying to reason with William just now was likely futile. Therefore, with an "if you say so" that clearly spoke of her disbelief, she and Jane left him and completed their turn of the garden before returning to the house – Jane to her room where she could wallow in misery undisturbed, and Elizabeth to her father's study.

~*~*~

"My Lizzy," he greeted her with a smile as she entered. "How might I be of service?"

Elizabeth settled into one of a pair of leather chairs in front of his desk. "I was wondering. Is it possible for a will to be ignored?"

"What do you mean?" Her father leaned forward. "Are you planning to contest my will?"

There was a teasing turn to his lips.

"Of course not!" Elizabeth replied. "I was just wondering about if someone were to leave, say, a set of dishes to his friend's niece and upon this someone's demise, the heir read the will but did not like this friend or his niece. Could he refuse to give the dishes to the niece?"

"Does the niece know about the bequeathing of the dishes?"

Elizabeth nodded.

"Then, I believe, she, or the agent acting on her behalf, would have grounds to protest, and the will would need to be executed as written. A will is a binding legal document. What it says must be carried out."

That was exactly what Elizabeth had thought. She only wished to be assured that she was thinking correctly.

"Was there anything else?"

She shook her head. "No."

"Then may I ask why you are inquiring after wills?"

Elizabeth had known he would be curious about that. "William and I were having a discussion about someone who has not done as instructed by his father's will, and I was certain that the will would have to be followed."

"Did he not give someone a set of dishes?" Her father's lips were still curled in amusement.

"No, it was a valuable living."

Her father's eyebrows rose, and his expression became serious. "Was a protest launched on this gentleman's behalf?"

Elizabeth scowled. She should have thought to ask William that. "I do not know."

Mr. Bennet leaned back. "If no protest was mounted, then I would be asking why it was not."

"Do you mean there could be a reason for the court to deny the gentleman his inheritance?" Again, she chided herself for not having thought of that in time to make mention of it to William.

"Why else would someone not attempt to gain what was rightfully his?" her father asked.

"I do not know," she answered honestly. There had to be a reason both for why Mr. Darcy had not given that man, whoever it was, the living and for why the man had not pursued the matter through the courts of law. Who would walk away from something that would provide him with the means to live, and quite comfortably, without at least attempting to pursue the matter in court? Of course, William had not said the case had not been taken to court, but if it had been and this man had not been installed in the living, then it would mean he had been denied by the court for some reason.

"It is then possible for a court to rule against a man attempting to claim his inheritance?" she asked.

"If there are conditions which must be met," her father replied.

"It is all very interesting and complex," Elizabeth muttered.

"Indeed, it is. That is why your uncle enjoys his work as he does. There is much to study, and your uncle has a keen wit, even if his wife does not."

Elizabeth chuckled.

"Of course, I should not jest but merely be thankful that a gentleman's intelligence is not judged by that of his wife."

"Papa!"

He winked at her. "I did not say I did not love your mother. However, she does drive me to distraction at times." He picked up the book he had discarded on his desk when Elizabeth had entered his study. "Was there anything else?"

"No, Papa. I think I know all I need to know."

"Was William right or wrong?" Her father called to her before she could close the door.

She poked her head around the door. "He was wrong, Papa." Very, very wrong.

Chapter 10

"Hurry," Elizabeth called to Jane as they walked out early on the Monday morning after the incident in the woods. "I do not wish to miss seeing Mr. Bingley go to the stables."

"Why could we not just go riding where you say he went on Saturday?" Jane called back.

"Because," Elizabeth stopped and waited for Jane to catch up with her, "Mr. Bingley might not take the same path every single day, and if we were to request our horses, we would likely have to explain to William why we did not wish to ride with him."

"Will he not think it strange for us to be walking in the field?"

"He will not ride in the field today. He has gone to Meryton to see the blacksmith."

"Then I do not understand why we could not

ride. It is not like we would be interested in visiting the blacksmith," Jane retorted.

She had a point. William would not expect them to join him on such an errand. When she was young, Elizabeth had enjoyed going to the blacksmith shop with her father and brother to see the fire and the glowing metal. However, she had long ago outgrown such a fascination.

"I thought it best to avoid William altogether," Elizabeth said. "Mr. Bingley has not yet called at Longbourn, and it is William's fault."

There, she had put voice to her anger. How William could keep Jane from an advantageous match such as Mr. Bingley posed, based on nothing more than mere gossip, Elizabeth could not fathom. For each of the past two evenings, she had subjected herself to poring over society pages with Lydia to make certain there was no mention of Mr. Darcy and secretly hoping that some bit of news about him might appear that would cause some doubt in the mind of her brother. However, the exercise had been for naught. There was nothing in the papers that could be remotely tied to Mr. Darcy – neither good nor bad. And yet, William seemed unrelenting in his position.

Their mother was beside herself with curiosity and had made several pleas to Mr. Bennet to call once again on Mr. Bingley and invite him to dinner. How were her daughters to make fine matches if he would not extend himself for them?

Each time Mrs. Bennet said such a thing, Elizabeth would skewer William with a pointed look to which he would only reply with a raised brow and an expression of being superior in his opinions. It was maddening. Elizabeth wanted to rail at him, but she would not, for she knew if she attempted to sway him in such a fashion in front of their parents, he would find it necessary to make his disapproval of both Mr. Darcy and Mr. Bingley known. As of yet, he had not shared what he knew with their father. Elizabeth knew he had not since she had asked him yesterday morning and again today when she saw him in passing in the upstairs hallway.

"He will relent with time," Jane said.

"He might," Elizabeth admitted, although she doubted it to be true, "but how long will that be? Will it be before Mrs. Long presents her daughter to Mr. Bingley? Or before Sir William invites him to dinner so he can meet Charlotte and Maria? We cannot risk such things, for although none can compare to you, how shall he ever know that unless he has spent time with you?"

"I do not like sneaking around."

"Who would be angry with us for staging a serendipitous meeting with Mr. Bingley on our walk?" Elizabeth asked. "Papa would chuckle, and Mama would be more than pleased to learn of such a scheme. It is only William who does not wish to see you well-matched."

Jane grasped Elizabeth's arm before she could lift her spyglass to her eye. "I do not wish to be the cause of a rift between you and William. You have been more than brother and sister. You have been friends. I do not wish to see that end."

Elizabeth shrugged. The thought pained her heart. She did consider William to be a friend and confidant. They had shared many secrets over the years. Even when he was at school, he had written to her about his friends and their antics – well, at least, some of them. She doubted he had told her everything since he had not mentioned hearing tales about Mr. Darcy. "He is wrong, Jane. I know he is. I asked Papa about the will. The living could not be refused simply because Mr. Darcy did not wish to give it to this person William met. If he will not listen to reason, then it is not you nor I who have caused a division. It is him and his unbending opinion."

Jane sighed. There was a sad resignation to the sound.

"We can make things right," Elizabeth assured her. "But to do so, we must talk to Mr. Bingley."

Those were the words that Jane needed to hear.

Elizabeth lifted her glass and scanned Netherfield's grounds.

Putting things right was something of which Jane could approve – even if doing so required a bit of subterfuge.

"He is halfway to the stables," Elizabeth said. "We will know if we are in luck shortly." She settled against the trunk of the tree and continued to watch the stables to see in which way Mr. Bingley would ride. With any luck, it would be toward the knoll and then to the left just as his route had been on Saturday.

As fortune would have it, Mr. Bingley appeared to be a creature of habit, and Elizabeth and Jane descended the knoll with plenty of time to slow their breathing and look at ease when he saw them.

Elizabeth lifted her hand and waved to him.

"He is not going to stop," Jane whispered.

"He will," Elizabeth whispered back as she waved a second time.

Mr. Bingley tipped his hat, and for a moment Elizabeth thought he would just ride on as Jane had said. However, he did not.

"Good morning, Mr. Bingley," Elizabeth said brightly as he drew near. "We are pleased to see you." She poked Jane with her elbow.

"Indeed, we are," Jane added.

"It is a pleasure to see you as well," Bingley replied.

Elizabeth noted how his eyes moved quickly from her to Jane and remained there. Jane ducked her head and smiled. She could box William's ears for keeping Jane and Mr. Bingley apart!

"There is a stile just over here," Elizabeth motioned toward the knoll. "I wish to speak with you."

Bingley's eyes shifted back to her. "You wished to speak to me?"

Elizabeth nodded. "About your friend."

He huffed.

"Please," Elizabeth entreated. "Is Mr. Darcy

well?" she asked cautiously. It seemed as if Mr. Bingley was angry with his friend and the indifferent shrug that accompanied his words suggested she was correct.

"He is, although he has been confined to his room for these two days."

"Will he be able to leave his room soon?" Jane asked.

Bingley smiled at her. "I believe he will be."

"Oh, I am glad," Jane replied.

Bingley swung down from his horse and walked the animal toward the stile where he secured him before crossing to where they stood waiting.

"I must thank you for sending the surgeon so quickly. I have yet to know the area well, although I did venture into Meryton on Saturday."

"How did you like it?" Jane asked.

"It is a fine town full of the friendliest sorts of people. Sir William has invited us to dine with him once Darcy is able to join us."

"Sir William is a delight," Jane said.

"Charlotte – Miss Lucas — is our particular friend," Elizabeth added as she shared a did-I-not-say-as-much look with Jane.

"But we did not ask you to join us to speak of our friends," Jane added quickly.

"No, according to Miss Elizabeth, you wished to know about my friend."

There as a decided note of bitterness in the word friend that caused Elizabeth to raise a brow. "We had hoped that you would call," she began.

Mr. Bingley's eyes fluttered, and shock suffused his features. "You did?"

"We did," Jane answered, again dipping her head and smiling.

"I thought I was not welcome." His brow was furrowed, and he shook his head slightly as if bewildered.

"I would welcome you."

Elizabeth wanted to shout and wrap her sister in an embrace for being so brave as to admit such a thing, for Jane was circumspect to a fault at times.

"You would?" Bingley could not contain the smile that spread across his face. "That is very good news."

"Indeed, it is," Elizabeth agreed quietly. A match between Jane and Mr. Bingley seemed almost assured if they could only sway William's opinion.

She waited patiently for a full minute as Mr. Bingley and Jane just looked at each other. Then, after coughing lightly, she said, "About Mr. Darcy."

"What do you wish to know?" Bingley asked eagerly, extending an arm to each of them.

"Is he betrothed?" Jane asked.

Bingley laughed. "No. Nor does he have much hope of ever becoming betrothed."

"Why would you say that?" Jane asked in surprise.

"Because he is too adept at offending," Bingley replied.

"Then he is cruel and cold?" Jane could not hide her horror at such a thought.

"No, no. He is just..." Bingley sought for the word.

"Ill-at-ease?" Elizabeth offered.

"Yes, yes! That is it precisely." He turned toward her. "I do not think I have ever met someone who has noticed that about my friend."

"Lizzy is very astute," Jane said.

"I would have to agree," Bingley replied. "Was there anything else you wished to know about Darcy?"

"Perhaps we could sit down," Elizabeth suggested.

Bingley agreed that it was a good idea and soon they were seated on the rise of the knoll.

"Our brother has not told me all he has heard about Mr. Darcy." Elizabeth smoothed her skirt over the top of her boots. "However, he has mentioned something about a will not being honoured."

"So, it was Wickham," Bingley muttered. He shook his head. "The will was honoured."

"Then, there was a reason for the living to not be given to this Wickham?" Elizabeth asked.

Bingley nodded. "He refused it, and Darcy paid him three thousand pounds in lieu of the living so that he could study the law. However, Wickham found that such study did not suit him, and when the living fell open, he came looking to claim it."

"But he had refused it," Jane said.

"Darcy reminded him of that fact. I am uncertain that Darcy will appreciate my sharing all of this with you, but since you asked." Bingley stretched out his legs and leaned back on his arms, looking for all the world as if he did not particularly care if Mr. Darcy would be happy with him or not. "Mr. Wickham was not in a favourable state of living at the time and was not pleased to be refused. He abused Darcy most severely and eventually retaliated in the cruelest fashion he could. That, I cannot tell you about other than to say Wickham's plan was designed to inflict the most pain possible to Darcy."

Elizabeth leaned toward Bingley. "Mr. Wickham was given three thousand pounds and was then shortly thereafter in need of money?"

Bingley nodded. "I should not likely say this to ladies, and I would not except to answer your question, but his proclivities are expensive."

"William did say he had played cards with him," Jane said.

"That is one of his vices," Bingley agreed. "As I understand it, his mother was a spendthrift, and I imagine he has inherited some of her traits in that area."

"Will Mr. Darcy be receiving callers soon?" Elizabeth asked, allowing the topic of Mr. Wickham to drop, although she had to admit to herself that she was curious to learn more. However, that was not the point of this discussion. This discussion was to promote her sister and to make it possible for Mr. Bingley to call on Jane without fear of being rejected by any of the men in her family.

Bingley looked at her in surprise. "I could not say with any certainty. May I ask why you wish to know?"

"I owe him an apology. I was demanding. It is a fault I own."

"He was rude," Bingley retorted.

"I am not saying he was not," Elizabeth replied. "I am only saying I was not right. Neither of us was shown to best advantage in that exchange. I should have considered the fact that he was injured more carefully and thought better of his comfort."

"You were thinking of his comfort. Riding to Netherfield did cause him a great deal of discomfort and swelling as you said it would."

"I am sorry to be correct," Elizabeth said, and she meant it. She had sprained an ankle more than once in her formative years as she tried to keep up with an older and larger brother. "However, I did not consider the comfort of his spirit. I would be very thankful if you would tell him of my sorrow in causing him discomfort."

Bingley smiled. "I suppose that will mean speaking to him." He shifted his position. "I will admit to being rather put out with him over his actions."

Elizabeth smiled. "I had thought you were."

"Did you?"

She nodded. "You did not seem willing to speak about him at first."

Bingley laughed. "Your sister is correct. You are most astute."

"Not always," Elizabeth assured him. "Will you call on us?"

"I do not know if that is wise."

"Our brother needs to see that you are as amiable as you appear," Elizabeth argued, "He would never promote any gentleman who was given to vice or who would in any way disrespect his family. Nor would he willingly accept a friend of such a gentleman. Therefore, you must call on us to show him that what he believes about Mr. Darcy cannot be true."

"And you would like me to call?" he asked Jane.

"Very much," she replied. This time, her head did not dip, but she did still smile and blush.

"Then I shall," he rose from the ground and extended a hand to Elizabeth first and then Jane to help them rise. "Today. I shall call today."

Elizabeth placed a hand on his arm as he turned to take his leave. "If you can think of any way to help us sway our brother's opinion of your friend..."

"I will give it some thought."

Elizabeth drew a breath and with her heart racing added, "I..." but then faltered. She was uncertain if she could be a brave as Jane had been. Jane, at least, had some evidence before her that Mr. Bingley would not be opposed to her declaration of interest. Elizabeth had nothing but the harsh words of an injured gentleman to propel her forward, but she knew she must not waiver. Mr. Bingley was looking at her, waiting patiently for her to continue.

"I should like very much for it to be possible for your friend to call at Longbourn, so that I might get to know more about him." She pushed the words out of her mouth before her brain had a chance to stop her.

Mr. Bingley smiled. "Then, I shall consider even more carefully how to sway your brother's opinion. And," he leaned a little bit closer to her and lowered his voice, "Darcy will definitely not approve of my saying this, but he shall be delighted to hear you would welcome him."

Elizabeth pulled the right corner of her bottom

lip between her teeth to keep from smiling too broadly.

"Truly?" Jane's voice was filled with poorly masked excitement.

"Truly." Bingley touched his hat and gave a small bow. "Until this afternoon," he said before turning and walking back to his horse.

Jane waited until he had tipped his hat to them and ridden away before she wrapped her arms around Elizabeth with a little squeal of delight. "Oh, your plan was brilliant!"

"Now it is brilliant? Earlier you did not seem to think it was."

"I was wrong," Jane said as they began their journey home. "Mama will be so delighted to have him call."

Yes, Mrs. Bennet would be pleased to have Mr. Bingley call at Longbourn, but not nearly so much as Jane or Elizabeth. For their happy futures appeared to not be outside the realm of possibilities – despite one foolish and stubborn older brother.

Chapter 11

Darcy descended the grand staircase at Netherfield slowly, one painful step at a time. His ankle was improving but placing weight on it was still difficult. Limping around a room with quick steps on a sore ankle as he had done for the past two days was not so bad as attempting to walk down a flight of stairs.

"Are you going somewhere?" Bingley, still dressed in his riding clothes, leaned against the wall at the bottom of the stairs.

How Darcy wished he could have gone for a ride this morning. He was so dreadfully tired of being confined to the house. He had had his fill of his room. However, to venture out of it meant being tended to by Louisa and Caroline, and Caroline seemed just as determined as ever to attempt to sway his mind in her direction. Riding would mean he would be free of both of Bingley's sisters, but it also meant his ankle would be jostled more than it should be. He had no desire to repeat having his boot become lodged on his foot due to swelling. Therefore, he had come to a decision. He was going...

"Home," Darcy replied.

"To town or Pemberley?"

"Town. I should l like to see my sister."

Bingley nodded. "Will you, at least, have tea with me before you leave?"

"Not unless you wish it." The man had not visited him in two days, and it was obvious from his expression that he was still not happy with Darcy. There was no way Darcy was going to impose on his friend if he was not welcome to do so.

"I do," Bingley replied, a small smile tipping his lips, giving away the fact that he was not as put out with Darcy as he pretended. "I do not wish for you to leave."

Darcy blew out a breath as he completed his journey to the bottom of the staircase and lowered himself onto the second step to rest his ankle before he proceeded any further.

"It still hurts?" Bingley nodded to Darcy's foot.

Darcy nodded. "It is not so strong as I would like it to be. I think it best to have my physician look at it when I am in town. Now that swelling has receded somewhat, he may see something that was missed before."

"You are determined to leave then?"

Again, Darcy nodded. "My remaining will only hinder any chance you have of securing Miss Bennet." He looked up at Bingley. "I did not do you harm intentionally, and I apologize for my temper."

Bingley extended a hand to Darcy. "Come. Have tea with me. I would like to speak with you."

Darcy looked at Bingley warily. "You would?" He allowed Bingley to help him rise from where he was seated.

"I would." He took Darcy by the arm. "Lean on me if you need to."

"Thank you," Darcy replied and did just that. He leaned his weight partially on his friend as they moved down the hall to a small withdrawing room behind the larger sitting room.

"Caroline does not like this room," Bingley whispered. "So, I have made it my own. It has only one smallish window and is therefore too dark for her liking. However, I do not mind the lack of sunshine so very much, especially if it brings with it a lack of sisters. I was about to eat some breakfast in here where it is free of female complaints when I was informed that your coach was being readied for travel." He locked the door behind him. "I want to make certain my sister does not interrupt me for I would like to eat in peace," he explained.

Bingley seated himself at a small round table that stood with four chairs near the window at the far end of the narrow room. There was a grouping of three cushioned chairs near the hearth and a ladder-backed chair near the door next to a cabinet which held a decanter and glasses. On the wall across from the fireplace, was a low bookcase with glass doors. Those pieces of furniture and a few paintings were the extents of the décor in the room. It was a very pleasant room. With the lamp lit, Darcy imagined this would be an excellent place to while away some hours with a book.

Darcy carefully took his place at the table. He was slowly learning how to sit down gracefully without causing his ankle too much discomfort. He was still a bit awkward, but not so awkward as he had been just yesterday morning.

"I saw Miss Bennet and Miss Elizabeth while I

was riding today," Bingley began as he poured tea for himself and Darcy.

"You did?" Darcy asked in surprise.

The left side of Bingley's lips tipped up, and his brows flicked upward and back down quickly. "I did. They were waiting for me."

Darcy added sugar to his cup. "It was not an accidental meeting?"

Bingley shook his head. "No, Miss Elizabeth wished to speak to me and arranged it so that she could. I am not entirely certain how she knew I would be riding where I was, but she and her sister were waiting and called to me to join them."

"Her brother must not know of this meeting," Darcy grumbled.

"You are correct. He does not." Bingley took a bite of his scone, following it with a bit of tea. "She asked about you."

"Who asked about me?"

"Miss Elizabeth."

Darcy could not help the small smile that crept onto his lips. Whether or not he had a hope of ever discovering if they would suit, he still found the information that she had inquired after him to be pleasing.

"She wanted to know if you are well enough for callers."

Darcy held his cup suspended in the air almost to his lips. "Is she thinking of calling on me?" What sort of lady called on a gentleman? It was supposed to be the other way around.

"She wishes to apologize."

Bingley's brows rose over an accusatory look, and Darcy sighed. "You are right, again. She is not the one who should apologize."

"I should say not," Bingley replied.

"Have you forgiven me?"

Bingley shrugged and nodded. "Tentatively, yes. However, if I never succeed with Miss Bennet, I retain my right to be put out with you." He held up a finger. "Which will mean that I will push you and Caroline together as much as necessary to have my regret somewhat mollified by your discomfort."

Darcy chuckled. "You are an evil man."

Bingley smiled broadly. "Far more evil than you imagine since I know that there is a pretty young lady to whom you need to apologize who would like nothing better than to have you call on her."

The sounds of the house, the ticking of a clock, the footsteps that scurried through the corridors, the nattering of the Bingley sisters as they descended the grand staircase faded into nothingness as the sound of the rhythmic thumping of Darcy's heart resounded in his ears. Miss Elizabeth wished for him to call on her? It could not be. He had been rude to her. She was not supposed to welcome him after he behaved as he had. If he were she, he would not wish to see him. He took two swallows of his tea and slowly returned his cup to the table as the sound of his heart diminished, and the room and Bingley came back into his consciousness.

"I do not deserve her," Darcy whispered. "She is too good."

No matter who might be associated with her brother, Darcy had not been able to talk himself out of wishing to know more about Elizabeth. She drew him as none other had ever done. That fact, mixed with not wishing to be confined to a house with Bingley's sisters and not wanting to remain where he was unwelcome, had been part of why he had planned to leave. To be near to someone so fascinating yet denied access to her presence for more than a few moments, if at all, was too torturous to contemplate. However, if he were in London, at least then, she would be too far away for him to regret not being able to call oh her as he wished with the intentions he could never make known or have accepted.

"You are correct," Bingley replied rather harshly. "She wished for me to convey her sorrow in having caused you discomfort. She said she should have considered your comfort of spirit – or some such thing." He placed his cup on the table and leaned toward Darcy. "You must pursue her even if you are not at this moment worthy of her." He held Darcy's gaze. "She understands you."

Darcy shook his head. No one understood him. Not at first. Sometimes not even after a long acquaintance.

"I know of what I speak," Bingley retorted. "When I told her you were not betrothed – because Miss Bennet had asked — and that you were likely never to become betrothed, Miss Bennet asked the reason. I told her that one of your many talents is in offending."

Darcy scowled at Bingley, but sadly, he was right. Darcy often found himself offending someone.

"While I was attempting to explain that you were not a heartless beast who offends because he gains pleasure from it, Miss Elizabeth suggested it was because you were ill-at-ease." Bingley's brows rose as he gave Darcy a pointed look. "Who, besides me, Richard, and Georgiana, realize that truth about you?"

"No one. Maybe my uncle."

Bingley nodded. "And Miss Elizabeth Bennet." He took a sip from his cup. "Marry her. There is likely not another woman in all of England who will understand that about you and still wish to have you call on her after you have been rude."

"That is a bit harsh," Darcy muttered. "True, but harsh."

Bingley popped the last of his scone in his mouth. "I am calling at Longbourn today. May I tell her that you will be riding tomorrow near the knoll?"

Darcy shrugged and nodded. "Yes?" He could risk the loss of a boot for such a reason, could he not?

"Capital decision," Bingley replied. "Shall I inform the staff that you are not departing?"

"Right. Yes." Darcy moved to stand up, but Bingley stopped him.

"Allow me to pull the bell. I told them some about Wickham," he added after ringing the bell.

"You did what?" Darcy asked.

"I told them about Wickham and the living he refused. Apparently, Mr. William Bennet has heard Wickham's tale of how he was mistreated by you. Miss Elizabeth, however, had deciphered that there must be a reason for the will to be ignored." Bingley looked at Darcy pointedly once again. "I repeat. Marry her."

Darcy chuckled and shook his head. "Did you tell them anything further about him?"

"I told them that he is given to vice and not to be trusted," Bingley replied. "But I did not tell them about Georgiana." He sighed. "Their brother is as protective of them as you are of your sister. He would not allow Wickham near them, nor will he welcome any gentleman who would disrespect his family in any way. Likewise, he will not accept the friend of such a gentleman. Therefore, it is imperative that we find a way to demonstrate to him that you are not the sort of gentleman to treat any of Bennet's family meanly. And that is why Miss Elizabeth was adamant that I call and do my part to show myself worthy of Miss Bennet – who, by the by, said she would welcome my attention."

"Congratulations," Darcy replied, and then after a moment to ponder Bingley's words, during which he considered his friend married to the sister of the only lady who had, to this point in his life, captured his attention as none other had ever done, he added, "Do not play with her emotions."

Bingley scowled at him. "I would not."

"No, I do not think you would, but you must appear to be above such since if you are found wanting, then I shall also be found wanting, seeing as I am your friend. That is, of course, if we can prove to the younger Mr. Bennet that I am not as reprehensible as my actions have accused me of being."

Bingley grinned. "You do not wish to be found wanting?"

Darcy shook his head. "I think your advice is excellent. I believe I must marry Miss Elizabeth."

Bingley laughed heartily at that. "I was beginning to wonder if there would ever be a day when I would hear you single out a lady." He filled his cup again. "No need to rush," he said. "We must attempt to come up with a way to secure the affections of the lady's brother, so that you and I will be free to pursue our happiness with his sisters."

~*~*~

Later that day, Darcy looked up from his book when Bingley entered the drawing room at Netherfield after his call at Longbourn.

"Caroline is not allowed to call at Longbourn in the future," he said, dropping into a chair next to Darcy.

"I do not see why I cannot," Caroline said with a smirk.

"Because you were rude, and I am attempting to make a good impression on Miss Bennet and her family. Telling Mrs. Bennet how her room is only half the size of some drawing room you sat in once to drink tea with some..." he pressed his lips together, obviously changing his mind on the word he was about to use, "ladies from the ton is not how one ingratiates herself to her neighbors. Nor should one tell a young lady such as Miss Lydia that the ribbon she is using to trim her hat is just like the one you saw last season." He glowered at his sister. "She seemed very flattered to have your attention until you condemned her fashion sense as already been done!"

"The call did not go well?" Darcy asked, attempting to thwart the upcoming argument, but it was to no avail. Caroline would have her say.

"I have no desire to become friends with *these* people, and you could do much better than Miss Bennet. Oh, she is a sweet girl to be sure and so pretty, but seriously Charles, what can she do for you?"

"Run my home! She is a gentleman's daughter and as such has first-hand knowledge about the workings of an estate and how one who is mistress of an estate should behave."

Caroline snorted. "I doubt her mother has taught her very well." She shared a look with Louisa. "Mrs. Bennet is not, how shall I say it?" She waved her hand in a circular fashion. "She is no wit."

Louisa bit her lip and looked at Bingley uneasily. "She does not seem to be, but we have only just met her."

Caroline huffed. "You know as well as I that she is not a glowing example of a gentlewoman, but then, she was not born to be one."

"Neither were you," Darcy said sharply, drawing the attention of everyone in the room. He never enjoyed one of Caroline's arguments with her brother. However, hearing her condemn the Bennets provoked him to the point that he could not remain silent.

"I may have been wrong before when I said there was no deficit in you which would cause me to reject you. You know very well how I regard ladies of the ton who are catty and cruel. I apparently did not realize that you were one of them."

Caroline gasped.

"You could be mistress of Longbourn," Charles inserted. "Then you could show Mrs. Bennet how a tradesman's daughter is supposed to run an estate. The young Mr. Bennet had a difficult time looking at anything else in the room save you. You could do far worse."

"And I could do better!" Caroline cried.

Bingley shrugged. "Perhaps."

"I could," Caroline insisted.

"You could," Darcy agreed. "However, I do not see how you will ever be happy with such a mean spirit. A gentleman of any status will have to interact with those who are not of his sphere as well as those just entering his sphere. He cannot afford to be petty and demeaning if he truly wishes to estab-

lish himself well and be respected. And if a gentleman cannot afford such behaviour, neither can
his wife. You have seen just as many troubled mar-
riages as I have. Being a demanding sort of lady and
prone to the ridicule of others does not bode well
for a peaceful marriage."

"Well said," Mr. Hurst said.

"Longbourn is not a horrid estate," Louisa
added. "Everything was tidy. That sitting room did
get excellent light, and from what I could see of the
garden, it must be spectacular when in full bloom."

"I did not like it," Caroline replied.

"You are well within your rights to not like what
others might," Mr. Hurst said. "However, those
opinions should be kept to one's self and only
delved into with caution when necessary to dis-
close them. For instance, I found the drapery to
be too garish, but I am not the one deciding on
the décor, and to be truthful, they were not out of
place."

Charles expelled a great breath. "I know you are
not pleased to be here, Caroline, but could you
please be reasonable and accept the fact that I like
it here and I like Miss Bennet? There is no need
to demonstrate your superior fashion sense or

schooling. It will be evident and better appreciated if you do not point it out."

"Miss Bennet?" There was a pleading tone to Caroline's voice.

"Yes, I prefer Miss Bennet to Miss Darcy — or to any other lady for that matter."

"You will not be moved?" Caroline asked.

The shake of Bingley's head was met by a resigned sigh. How many times had Darcy witnessed these two argue over something? Caroline would petulantly pursue her brother to change his mind until it became clear that he would not be moved. Then, and only then, did she resign herself to the idea – albeit unhappily.

"I will not be marrying Georgiana, and Darcy will not be marrying you. Therefore, you should begin searching for another, and you could start with Mr. William Bennet. He seems very upstanding."

"I have no hope?" The question to Darcy was small and quiet.

"I am sorry, but no," Darcy replied.

Caroline sighed again and pushed up from her chair. "Then, I see no need to stay here if I can neither move Charles or impress you. I am a very accomplished lady."

"I know," Darcy replied. "And some gentleman will be happy to have you for his wife, but that gentleman is not me."

She shrugged and moved to the door of the drawing room where she stopped and turned toward them once again. "I apologize for being less than civil, Charles. I shall attempt to display myself to better advantage and make our sojourn in this backwater as pleasant as possible."

"I am happy to hear it, but Darcy'll not marry you even if you are pleasant."

She huffed. "I was not attempting to sway him."

"You were not?" Hurst asked with a laugh.

Caroline paused a moment too long before replying in the negative to Mr. Hurst for either him or her brother to believe her answer.

"Give him up," Charles said.

Caroline lifted her chin and shot him a hateful look before saying, "I already have," and leaving the room.

"Miss Elizabeth will be walking near the knoll tomorrow morning," Bingley said to Darcy.

"Oh ho!" Mr. Hurst cried. "You'll want to prepare your sister for that disappointment," he said to his wife.

Darcy shook his head and glared at Bingley. "We are even," he growled.

Bingley laughed. "As long as I succeed with Miss Bennet."

"No, even if you do not," Darcy retorted. Then, he turned to Mrs. Hurst. "It is as your husband suspects, so it would be best for Caroline to treat Miss Elizabeth with respect and kindness should she wish to keep my acquaintance."

Chapter 12

Elizabeth paced along the fence from the stile to the bottom of the knoll just down and to the right of the tree she liked to sit under. She glanced up at the sky. The sun was shining, and the clouds were nearly white. There was only a hint of grey in them. The day should be a dry one.

She opened her book and attempted to make her mind focus on the words. She had brought it with her even though she had not intended to read today. To leave without it and go toward her favorite reading place might have caused some to be curious – William in particular. He had been just leaving for the stables when she had descended the stairs with her pelisse and bonnet on.

She snapped the book closed. It was no use. All she could think about was Mr. Darcy. He had plagued her dreams all night. Hopefully, he would be receptive to her apology and willing to help her convince her brother that neither he nor Mr. Bingley was reprehensible.

"Miss Elizabeth."

Elizabeth spun from her contemplation of the trees and her dreams, where the man presently calling to her had at one point forgiven her and another, ridiculed her for her demanding nature. Her heart thumped loudly as she moved toward the stile.

"Good morning!" she called to him. "I am delighted to see you are able to ride. Mr. Bingley said you had found your confinement to be trying." She kept a smile on her face and her tone light. Even as her stomach tumbled nervously.

"It was excessively trying," he said as he swung down from his horse.

Elizabeth bit her lip to keep from telling him to be careful as he winced while putting weight on his ankle. "Can you make it over the stile? We can sit in the shade." She motioned to her right.

"I think I can manage it," he replied. "It cannot be any more difficult than descending a set of stairs or mounting a horse. It is amazing the movements upon which we rely and about which we do not think until some portion of our person is incapacitated in some fashion."

"You can lean on me if you need." Elizabeth pressed her lips together. She had told herself she would not try to direct him in any fashion today, but it was much harder than she had imagined it would be. And she had considered that it would be difficult.

He smiled. "It is healing, so I think I can manage. However, when we must rise from our places later, I may require assistance."

Elizabeth expelled the breath she has been holding.

"Before you say what I suspect you are going to say," Darcy said as they walked the few feet to where she and Jane had sat with Bingley just the other day. "I must insist that it is not you who needs to beg forgiveness. My behavior was reprehensible."

"You were injured," she replied. "We can all become cantankerous when in pain. We can sit here. Do you need help?"

He shook his head. "No, I think I can drop onto

the ground under my own power, though it will not be gracefully done." And it was not.

"Are you well?" she asked in response to the groan he uttered.

"I am." He stretched out his injured leg but kept his other leg bent. "An injury does not excuse my lack of patience."

She shrugged. "It is not an excuse. It is a reason. There is a difference, Mr. Darcy. One attempts to brush something away as if it should be overlooked completely while the other is given in hopes of making a situation or action understandable. I should have considered your injury when proffering my advice –"

"Which was sound, by the way," Darcy inserted. "I nearly lost my boot."

"Could we begin again? Neither of us showed ourselves to best advantage."

He shook his head, and Elizabeth's heart clenched at the thought of their not being able to reconcile the ill behaviour displayed at their last meeting.

"I would prefer," he said, "to continue as we have been, for I would have you know that I can be dour and disapproving at times. It is a fault I willingly own, and I do not wish to present myself to you as anything that I am not." He removed his hat and placed it on the ground next to him. "I would rather begin by knowing you are an intelligent lady who is not put off by my occasional fits of spleen. I think whatever relationship we might foster will be better for the transparency. It is one of the things I despise about the season – there are so few who are what they appear."

Relief that he was not going to send her on her way but would rather be friends spread across Elizabeth's face. "You may come to regret such a request," she teased. "I can assure you that I have many faults of temper, and one of them is my insistence that I know the best way to do things, and another is my tendency to express my annoyance when others do not immediately agree."

Darcy chuckled. "We are much alike then. Am I forgiven?"

She nodded. "Am I?"

"Without a moment's hesitation," he replied. He shifted so that he could see her more fully as she sat beside him.

Oh, he was handsome! From where she had seen him on his horse on their first meeting and then on the ground in the woods, she had thought him very attractive, but now that he was here, so close to her with his hat removed and looking very relaxed, he was even more appealing.

"I understand Mr. Bingley told you somewhat about Mr. Wickham."

"Yes, he did," she said, pulling her eyes away from the cut of his jawline and blushing.

"Is your brother a good friend of Mr. Wickham?"

Elizabeth shook her head and shrugged. "I do not believe he is. He had never mentioned him before I questioned him about his opinion of you. Indeed, he did not mention his name even then. I dare say, Mr. Wickham is no more than a passing acquaintance."

"I am glad to hear it."

His broad shoulders rose and lowered as he drew a deep breath and expelled it. "It was not entirely my injury that made me cross that day in the wood. I had just discovered that your brother knew Wickham."

He shook his head and looked past her, a pained expression settling into his eyes. "Your brother asked me if I was betrothed but said he had not met any of my family. There was only one other person of whom I could think who would know such information."

"Mr. Wickham?"

Darcy nodded. "He was a childhood friend."

"What happened?" Her hand flew to cover her mouth. "I apologize. It is not my place to know."

His smile was soft and reassuring. "I would like for you to know every last thing there is to know about me, and I would like to know the same about you if you are willing to be so open."

Her lips parted of their own accord as her brow furrowed. Was he saying what she thought he was saying?

"Yes," he replied to her unspoken question. "I think you and I would suit each other very well, and I would like to explore the possibility of our compatibility not just as friends but as future mates."

For a full three deafening thuds of her heart, Elizabeth could not find anything more to say than "oh."

"Would you be willing to consider me as more than a friend?"

After having only met twice – with one of those times being nothing more than an argument — he wished to court her? "Do you always make such hasty decisions, Mr. Darcy?

He chuckled. "No. I rarely do anything in haste. However, you and your enchanting eyes and smile have not given me a moment of peace since we met. I find I am as anxious to know about you as a man is for a drink of water in the desert. I cannot explain it. I just know that I must discover all I can about you."

"You are certain you wish this?"

He nodded.

"I apologize for my hesitance, but I am not the sort of lady whom gentlemen trip over one another to call on."

"Then, they are fools. Will you?"

She laughed. "Yes. I would consider it an honour to enter into such an arrangement." She could feel the heat of embarrassment climbing onto her cheeks. "I must admit that I have found myself fascinated by you."

"You have? How so?"

"You think deeply."

"I do, but how do you know that?"

The surprise in his tone caused her to smile. "There is a small twitch of your eyes or lips and a pause before you speak. You looked very pensive on our first meeting."

"Bingley said you were astute."

How she wished that were always true, but she knew that she often leapt to conclusions and held to her beliefs about a person or situation to be true, even when they were not. In that way, she and William were alike, and she could see very clearly at this moment how that tendency was harmful. "I wish it were always true. I do attempt to decipher character, but I am not always correct."

"No one is," he replied. "I have made some griev-ous errors in that regard." He plucked a blade of grass and ran it back and forth between his fingers. "I wish to tell you something, but I confess to being fearful." He blew out a breath. "However, I have promised to reveal myself to you as fully as I can."

"You do not have to tell me if it is painful." How wrong her brother was about this gentleman! He was not cold or cruel. He might be irascible at times, but Mr. Darcy was not unfeeling.

"I feel I must, but before I do, I must beg you not to speak of this to anyone as doing so might harm someone who is very dear to me."

Her heart clenched at the look on his face. What

he was willing to tell her was excruciating, and she could not deny the honour of being so trusted. "Of course, I will not say a word."

"Thank you," he said with a small smile before finding some spot beyond her at which to look and proceeding to tear the blade of grass in his hands to shreds as he told her about his sister, Georgiana's, narrow escape from a life of misery at the hands of Mr. Wickham.

"We, my cousin and I, were both mistaken in the character of Georgiana's companion, Mrs. Younge. We had no idea that she was an associate of Wickham." He sighed. "That is why I was so cross when I discovered your brother's acquaintance with Wickham. I thought I had once again misjudged someone's character, and I feared that if I were correct about your brother, it would mean never being able to know you. It was as if Wickham was attempting to tear yet another thing away from me. He claimed my father's affections, nearly robbed me of my sister, and then, when I finally met a lady who captured my interest and, I feared, my heart, he was there again."

Elizabeth brushed a tear from her cheek. "I do not know what to say," she muttered.

He turned his attention back to her and immediately fished in his pocket for his handkerchief. "I did not mean to distress you."

She shook her head. "You must not apologize for telling me about Mr. Wickham. If my brother knew, he would never give a word the man told him a second thought. I will not tell him," she added quickly when she noted the look of concern in Darcy's eyes. "I have given you my word. I am just assuring you that my brother would never be friends with such a man."

For a few moments, the sound of the breeze rustling dry leaves and a bird chirping were all that could be heard as they sat in companionable silence. It was strange to Elizabeth how right it seemed to be sitting here with him, bearing a small portion of his cares. She glanced at him. His head was tipped back slightly as he watched the clouds. She would not be opposed to being his wife. In fact, the thought was rather intoxicating, much like the small smile that curved his lips, for he seemed to be precisely the sort of gentleman who would best suit her. He willingly owned his faults, cared deeply for his sister, and had presented himself to her in a very direct fashion. All of those things spoke to a strength and nobility of character that made the idea of being married to him something to be sought happily without a moment's pause to worry about her future happiness. With him, she just knew that she would be happy. She smiled and shook her head. It was just as he had said – it was a realization that defied understanding.

"My brother is not really my brother," she said breaking the silence.

"I beg your pardon?" Darcy turned toward her.

"I do not have any grievous tales to share, but you should know that William is a distant cousin and heir to Longbourn, whose father died when he was ten, and he was sent to live with us. He has since become more of a brother than a cousin. In fact, he and I have been good friends nearly from his arrival."

"It is not easy to lose a parent whether you are young or old."

She chided herself. He had just told her he was the guardian of his younger sister. He would not be her guardian if his parents lived. "How long have your parents been gone?" she asked quietly.

"My mother died when I was but a boy and my

father just five years ago." He smiled at her. "Too old to be taken in by a loving family. Your brother is fortunate."

She returned his smile. "He is, and if we can convince him that you are not the ogre you appeared, then.." she swallowed the fear that rose in her throat. If Jane could be brave, she reminded herself, surely, she could be as well. "One day, perhaps you could also become part of our family?"

Any fear that might have fluttered in her stomach was dashed away by the bright grin that overtook his face. "I would like that very much." He shifted his position. "As much as I would like to sit here all day with you, I fear it is not a good idea. For one, my stomach is about to become very boisterous, and for another, your brother might come looking for you. That would not aid us in our quest to sway his opinion."

Elizabeth pushed up to her feet, straightened her skirts, and blushed when she realizes she was the subject of Mr. Darcy's close scrutiny. She held out her hand to him. "Try not to topple me," she teased. "I should like to be able to dance every set at the assembly, and I fear there might not be enough time to heal if I should injure myself."

"I would not dream of causing you pain," he replied lightly as he took her hand and pushed up from his position, using only his strong leg as much as he could. "If my ankle is better by then, perhaps I will be fortunate enough to claim one of your sets?"

"Oh, two sets would set Mama up proudly," Elizabeth replied with a laugh. "It will also likely shock her unless we have been able to move our meetings from clandestine locations to more standard surroundings for a gentleman to call on a lady."

He tucked her hand in the crook of his arm as they walked the short distance to where his horse was enjoying a wildflower. "With your permission, I would like to accompany my friend when he calls on your sister."

"I would like that very much, but William will not be welcoming."

"I know, and I cannot blame him. I would be far from welcoming to anyone who called on Georgiana after treating her as I treated you – especially if I believed him to be as Wickham has painted me to be." He lifted her hand to his lips before crossing the stile. "We will sway him. We must."

Elizabeth stood at the stile for an extended

period of time after Darcy rode away. He liked her. The handsome new neighbour's much more handsome friend liked her. She shook her head. It was wonderfully unbelievable. Finally, when she could see him no longer, she retrieved her book and returned to Longbourn.

Chapter 13

For two days, Darcy endured the glares and huffs of William Bennet as he sat with Elizabeth in the sitting room at Longbourn. Each day, he had also enjoyed a few glare-free moments in Elizabeth's company as he would stop at the knoll each morning where she was waiting for him. He had learned a good deal about her in a short time.

Her mother was not the source of Elizabeth's intelligence. Caroline had been correct about Mrs. Bennet not being a wit. However, he could see that in her strange and loud way, she was a caring mother, intent upon seeing her daughters married. In that way, she was no different from any of the mothers, as well many of the father and brothers, of the ton. They all wanted to see their sisters and daughters married and married well. He could not fault Mrs. Bennet for that desire. He did struggle with enjoying her boisterous nature, but then, he struggled with that trait in all people.

Elizabeth had been raised in a good household. It may have been wanting in some ways – such as exposure to the masters – but it was not lacking in love. That was clearly evident. Mr. Bennet, while not always present and often quiet when he was in company, had quick eyes. He might look as if he were reading a paper, but Darcy had seen the man silently watching both him and Bingley. Thankfully, Elizabeth's father, unlike his son, wore a pleasant expression when observing and had not told either him or Bingley that they could not call. If William had spoken to his father about anything that Wickham had told him, it did not appear that it was something which would hinder Darcy's acceptance when he finally approached the gentleman about a proper courtship and marriage.

On the third day after Darcy and Elizabeth had come to their understanding at the bottom of the knoll, Darcy found himself and Bingley invited to dine at Longbourn. Happily, he dressed in his best suit of clothes and entered the carriage. He and Bingley intended to arrive early so that they could speak privately with Mr. Bennet before they ate.

"Are you certain before dinner is the best time?" Bingley asked.

"No," Darcy admitted. "But I should like to have the interview over with before our evening begins, no matter the outcome."

"We could be asked to leave." Bingley fidgeted with his sleeves as he sat in Darcy's carriage. The Hursts and Caroline would arrive later in Bingley's carriage.

Darcy nodded. He did not need to be reminded of the fact that he might be unsuccessful. He had no fear about his acceptance from Elizabeth. She had given that to him this morning. He smiled as he remembered holding her in his arms and the softness of her lips against his own.

"You look far too happy for the situation," Bingley muttered.

"I am attempting to think about pleasant things," Darcy replied.

"Such as?" Bingley prompted with an air of skepticism.

"A pair of fine eyes," Darcy replied with a smile.

Bingley chuckled.

"And soft lips," Darcy added.

Bingley's eyes grew wide. "You have kissed her?"

Darcy shrugged. "I did not say that I have."

"Out with it." Bingley bumped Darcy's uninjured foot with his.

"It was this morning when I asked her if she would allow me to speak to her father even though her brother has not relented in his position, and after she had given me permission to do so, she also gave me permission to kiss her," Darcy said.

Bingley shook his head and chuckled. "I never expected you to beat me to it."

"You intend to kiss Miss Elizabeth?" Darcy teased.

"Obviously not!" Bingley said with a laugh. "You have gained the acceptance of a lady before I have even asked."

"We cannot all be so decisive," Darcy quipped.

Bingley continued to chuckle. "I hope then that we are successful with her father, or you will be plagued by the memory of that kiss far more than I will be distressed about never having gotten one from Miss Bennet."

Darcy drew and released a breath. Whether he was successful or not, that kiss was likely to plague him until he could claim another. "We must succeed" was all he said before the carriage fell into silence for the short distance that remained of their three-mile journey from Netherfield to Long-bourn.

"Is the master available?" Darcy asked Mr. Hill when he opened the door to them.

The elderly servant's lips curled up in a small smile, and the skin around his eyes crinkled with delight. "He is in his study. I will inquire if he is willing to see you, Mr. Darcy."

"And Mr. Bingley," Bingley added.

"And Mr. Bingley," Mr. Hill amended. "Wait here, I will return shortly."

"Perhaps we should have waited," Darcy muttered as the urge to flee suddenly took hold of him. The fear of his petition being denied settled into his stomach and caused his heart to race.

"It is far too late to decide that now," Bingley chided.

"I know," Darcy said as he tugged at his jacket. "We will succeed."

"Of course, we will," Bingley assured him, although to Darcy it did not sound as if Bingley were very sure of their success.

"Oh, Mr. Darcy, Mr. Bingley," Mrs. Bennet said

as she descended the stairs, "why are you standing here instead of sitting within?"

"We were waiting on Mr. Hill," Bingley answered.

"Waiting on Mr. Hill? For what?" Mrs. Bennet asked. "Hill," she said as the servant approached them, "why are these men waiting for you?"

"The master will see you," Mr. Hill said to Darcy and Bingley.

Mrs. Bennet gasped. "You wish to see Mr. Bennet?"

"Yes, ma'am," Bingley answered.

"Indeed, we do," Darcy added.

"Well! Do not let me detain you!" she cried in delight and moved toward the sitting room. "Perhaps we will have a bottle of claret with our dinner?" she asked, turning back toward them when she was just outside the sitting room.

"Perhaps," Darcy replied with a tight smile while he hoped that there would be a happy reason for imbibing.

Darcy's heart thumped loudly with each of the few steps to Mr. Bennet's study. He paused only a moment to pull in a fortifying breath and to remind himself of his need to succeed before entering the room.

"Gentlemen," Mr. Bennet waved them to the chairs before his desk, "Mr. Hill informs me that you wish to speak to me."

"We do," Darcy said as he took his seat. The room felt very warm at present even with only the presence of a few glowing embers in the grate.

"I will assume it is about my daughters."

Darcy silently thanked the Lord for allowing the gentleman to broach the subject, so that he did not have to. "Yes, sir. I would like to marry Miss Elizabeth."

Bingley looked at him with wide eyes, and for good reason. Marry was not the word that was supposed to have come out of his mouth. It was supposed to be court.

"I mean to say, I should like permission to court Miss Elizabeth with the intent of eventually marrying her." Darcy rubbed his hands on his breeches and forced his lungs to fill with air.

Mr. Bennet chuckled. "I assume you have never done this before?"

Darcy's brow furrowed. Why would he have done this before? Offering to court and marry someone was not something a gentleman did on a regular basis, was it?

Mr. Bennet continued to chuckle. "I am teasing you, Mr. Darcy. These requests are not easy for any of us to make." He turned his eyes toward Bingley, who gulped.

"I would like to court Miss Bennet," Bingley said.

"To what end?"

Bingley blinked.

"Do you also wish permission to marry her?" Mr. Bennet asked.

To Darcy, it looked as if the man was enjoying their discomfort far too much. Of course, he was not about to point that out.

Bingley nodded eagerly. "Of course. Yes. I would like to marry her if that is her wish after we have come to know each other better."

"Is there any reason I should deny either of you?"

Darcy began to shake his head but then stopped. "There is one reason."

Again, Bingley turned wide eyes to him.

"Your son will not approve of either of us. I was

rude to Miss Elizabeth when she came upon me after I had injured myself."

Mr. Bennet's brow furrowed. "She has welcomed you since, so I am going to assume that either you have been forgiven or your rudeness was not such that it angered her. For I know my daughter is not one to allow rudeness to pass without some exchange of words."

"You are correct," Darcy said. "She has forgiven me, but..."

"William has not."

"No, he has not, but for reasons that go beyond my behaviour on that morning in the wood."

Mr. Bennet's head tipped, and he studied Darcy with curiosity. "What reasons might he have? I know he has not seemed welcoming of you since he learned your name."

Darcy blew out a breath. "He has been told some things about me that are not true. However, the person who shared these lies with him is convincingly charming, and then when I replied crossly to Miss Elizabeth, Mr. William Bennet took that as proof that what he had heard was correct."

Mr. Bennet's head bobbed up and down slowly.

"Would this have anything to do with a will not being executed as written?"

"Yes, sir."

"That explains why Lizzy was asking me about wills." He sighed. "She seemed very determined to prove your innocence. I think you will have no trouble convincing her to accept you." He grimaced. "However, her brother will be more challenging. I thought I had met the most obstinate child when Elizabeth was born, but then William arrived." He shook his head. "He is exceptionally hard to move at times – especially if he thinks his family, Lizzy in particular, has been injured. His opinion once lost is most challenging to restore."

"I understand. I am the same."

Mr. Bennet chuckled. "That is good to know. Such obstinacy will stand you in good stead when dealing with Elizabeth." He smiled. "You both have my permission to present your offers to my daughters, and I will make my son aware of the fact that I find no reason to prevent you. Of course, I will expect a call regarding all the financial particulars once you have come to the point."

"Thank you," Bingley said happily.

"Yes, thank you, sir," Darcy said. "Both for your

permission and believing me to be as I appear – for I assure you I am."

Mr. Bennet stood. "My Lizzy would not defend you so strongly if you were anything other than honorable. She saw the error in the tale she had been told and ferreted out the information she needed to be assured that her opinion of you was correct. Therefore, it is not I but Elizabeth who deserves your thanks on that front. However, since she is not here, I will take it." He chuckled and moved around his desk.

"I think I will wait to tell my wife the good news," he said. "She will be overjoyed, of course, but her joy can become excessive."

"She met us in the entry," Bingley said.

Mr. Bennet sighed. "Then there is no hope for you now. I suggest you speak to my daughters directly or the whole business shall be decided and proclaimed by their mother."

And they did just as he said, securing their ladies during a stroll in the garden before dinner.

As it turned out, dinner was a somewhat painful experience for Darcy. Mrs. Bennet was overjoyed just as her husband had said she would be, and

William seethed with anger exactly as Darcy had expected he would.

Thankfully, William had kept his opinions to himself for the entire evening and did not created a scene or put voice to his displeasure while in company. However, as Darcy was leaving, William had approached him, which was why Darcy now stood at the edge of the field near the knoll as the sun was rising, waiting for William to appear for their appointment.

Darcy sliced the air with his foil and shuffled through a position or two. His foot was hurting, but not so much that it made him concerned about having a great disadvantage. What did concern him regarding disadvantages was William's reach. Darcy was certain that the younger Mr. Bennet's arms were longer than his, which would make it far easier for him to land his points.

"This is ridiculous," Bingley said.

"I agree," Darcy replied. "But he demanded satisfaction for having his wishes ignored. It will change nothing. It will only make him feel he has gotten redress."

"He believes lies!" Bingley fairly shouted. "And

he is challenging you to defend your honour without bothering to ask you about what he has heard!"

Darcy sighed. "I realize what he is doing and that it is foolish, but I also believe he will be more willing to listen after he has expended some of his anger."

"At your expense!"

Darcy nodded, and Bingley paced a circuit near the fence, muttering to himself about foolishness and how the weather was growing decidedly more chilled each morning.

It was only about five minutes later that William Bennet arrived with Mr. Bennet.

"I would not allow him to find another to stand with him," Mr. Bennet explained. "I have no desire to have this foolishness broadcast far and wide." He leveled a glare at his son.

"He is not what he seems," William replied.

"So you have said, repeatedly. However, I have yet to learn if you have discussed that with him." Mr. Bennet replied.

"No, he has not," Bingley answered.

"Good morning, Mr. Bingley. I can see you are as pleased as I am to be here."

"Indeed." Bingley crossed his arms and scowled at William.

"Shall we begin?" Darcy asked.

"I applaud your ability to be so calm," Mr. Bennet said to Darcy.

Darcy only smiled grimly. His calmness was a façade. Within, he was incensed that William Bennet was so stubborn as to act before thinking. That quality did not recommend him to Darcy. He could understand the man's need to protect his sisters, but he could not comprehend doing so in such an ignorant fashion.

Mr. Bennet chuckled at Darcy's response and nodded his understanding. "Let me amend that. I applaud your control."

Bingley stepped between Darcy and William. "You will cede the field when you have been hit three times." He raised a brow and glared at William. "He is injured, and I'll not let him suffer for longer than that."

William gave a nod of his head. And then, when Bingley had stepped back, the duel began.

"What are you doing?" Elizabeth shouted from the top of the knoll before running down to where her father was.

"William feels he was injured in some fashion because Mr. Darcy dared to pursue you after William had told him he was not welcome."

"And you condone this?" she asked her father in surprise.

He shook his head. "I did not want him bringing anyone else into the situation, so I insisted that I be the one to attend him and see that things were done fairly."

"You!" Elizabeth turned on William, who had stopped his match with Darcy and was standing, waiting to resume. "You would question our father's decision? You would question my ability to choose wisely?" She spat the questions at her brother as she advanced toward him. "How could you?"

"He has fooled you," William replied.

"The only fool is you!" Elizabeth cried. "You have no support of your beliefs other than a few cross words spoken by an injured man."

"I know what I have heard," William ground out. "I have no desire to see you tied to such a man as I have heard Mr. Darcy to be."

"I have already accepted him."

"It can be undone." William pulled himself straight.

"You are being ridiculous!" Elizabeth threw her hands up in exasperation.

"That is precisely what I said," Bingley agreed.

"I am being as I should be," William shot back. "I am trying to protect you just as you asked me to."

"Stop!" Elizabeth brushed tears from her cheek. "Just stop."

Darcy longed to go to her, to comfort her, but he also knew that in so doing, he would only provoke her brother further.

"I will stop if you will undo what you have done."

Elizabeth gasped and looked from her brother to her father and back.

"William," Mr. Bennet said sharply, "consider carefully what you are asking. I have given my permission. I see no reason to refuse a man like Mr. Darcy."

William looked nowhere but at Elizabeth. "What is your answer?"

"You are truly asking me to chose between you and Mr. Darcy?"

William nodded.

Elizabeth shook her head.

Darcy forced himself to stay where he was instead of thrashing William as he deserved. If he were ever to win over Elizabeth's brother, it would not be with force or apparently logic.

"I love you," Elizabeth's eyes shifted from William to Darcy. "Both of you." She held Darcy's gaze for a heartbeat or two before she shrugged sadly and turned back to her brother. "But," she wiped tears from her face with the palm of her hand, "I choose him. I choose Mr. Darcy."

For the briefest of moments, Darcy wanted to shout his victory to the sky. Elizabeth loved him enough to choose him above her brother. However, in a flash as powerful and quick as lightning, his elation was dashed to grief for he knew what he had to do. "No."

All eyes turned toward him.

"I cannot allow it." He moved toward Elizabeth. "I will not take you from your brother no matter how dear you are to me. I would be no better than Wickham if I did. He has always taken what he wanted without regard for those around him." He shook his head. "No that is not true. He has taken

what he wanted where I am concerned while rel-
ishing in the pain it caused me."

Elizabeth shook her head. Her tears increasing
and tearing at Darcy's heart.

Mr. Bennet stepped over to where he was. "But
in refusing Elizabeth's choice are you not allowing
the stories this Wickham has told to take her from
you?"

Darcy swallowed against the tears he could feel
threatening and nodded. "But I will not be what he
is. He nearly claimed my sister this past summer,
and my desolation would have been complete. I
cannot be the source of such pain for another."

"But what of Elizabeth?" Mr. Bennet asked
softly.

That was a touch too far for Darcy's composure.
"I will," his voice cracked, and a tear escaped down
his cheek. "Wait for her," he finished in a whisper.
"For as long as it takes." He bowed to William and
Mr. Bennet, pressed a kiss to Elizabeth's hand and
quickly found his horse and took his leave before
either his resolve crumbled, or he made an utter
fool of himself by weeping.

Chapter 14

Through her tears, Elizabeth watched Mr. Darcy, followed by Mr. Bingley, go. Her father wrapped her in his arms.

"I thought there was little danger in your brother meeting with Mr. Darcy, or I would have forbidden it."

Elizabeth had no words. All she was capable of doing at present was shaking her head. It was not his fault that Mr. Darcy had left her.

"Come," he said gently. "You may ride my horse, and I will walk beside you."

"No," she managed to force from her lips.

"You cannot stay here," said William.

She pushed away from her father and turned toward her brother. "Do not speak to me!" She blew out a breath. "Ever," she added. "I did not choose you, nor will I ever. And I will not return to the house with you!" Fury such as she had never felt rose within her. How could he be so stupid as to not see that Mr. Darcy was a perfectly honorable gentleman?

"Lizzy," her father said softly, "you will eventually have to speak to William."

She shook her head.

Mr. Bennet sighed. "I will send Jane to you. You will be under your tree?"

Elizabeth nodded.

"I do not want Jane to have to wander hither and yon trying to find you," he cautioned.

"I will be where you said." She drew a sleeve of her pelisse across her eyes in an attempt to dry her tears, not that, at this moment, she thought they would ever stop flowing.

"Will you accept both my handkerchief and that of your brother?" Mr. Bennet held out his handkerchief to her as William withdrew his from his pocket.

Gratefully, Elizabeth took the piece of cloth from her father but hesitated before accepting William's. She did not wish to even touch something which belonged to him at present, but she did have need of something to dry her eyes and nose. She murmured a thank you and turned to leave them and go to her tree.

"Lizzy," William called after her. She could hear his concern for her in his voice, and despite her anger, it pricked her heart.

"Do not speak to me," she threw the words over her shoulder. Then she stopped. She would not listen to him, but he could listen to her. Perhaps now he would be more willing to do so. "You know nothing of him! Nothing! When you know about him. When you can tell me all you know about him which you have heard from his own lips – not from the lips of another profligate schemer – " she smiled at his look of shock at her choice of words. "—only then, will I allow you to speak to me."

And with those words, she turned away once more and made her way to where she could attempt to gain control of her sorrow. She could not return to the house and her mother as she was right now. She would need to gather some semblance of fortitude before facing her mother's concerned coddling.

She sank down under the tree, heedless of her gown or pelisse. Not much seemed worthy of consideration presently. She pulled her knees up and rested her forehead on them as she allowed herself to fully indulge in the misery of her heart. She berated William for his actions for several minutes until her anger was spent. Then she turned her thoughts to Mr. Darcy.

She lifted her head and looked toward Netherfield. "I love you," she whispered. She had not known it until she had been met with William's demand. She had known she admired Mr. Darcy and that she longed to know more about him. She had known that she wished for him to take her hand and, she smiled through her tears, she had known when he kissed her that she would like to have him do so again. But in the instant when she had to choose between giving him up and remaining as she had always been or stepping away from the familiar confines of her family to be at his side, she had come to realize just what it was that drew her to him. It was not his wealth or his handsome features. It was him – his heart, his character, the way he smiled when he saw her, the ease with which they entered into intimate conversation – it was who he would be even if all his riches were removed and his features, disfigured. And she had known that she could not give him up any more than she could hand William her own heart.

How such a love had developed in so short a time was beyond her comprehension. But then, it did not matter how it happened. It only mattered that it had and now it been torn from her.

She buried her head in her arms which still rested on her knees and wept without thinking for a few moments. Then, determined that she would not be a complete watering pot when Jane arrived, she lifted her head, dried her tears, and attempted to keep more from spilling as she replayed the events of the morning in her head. She had been so excited to see Mr. Darcy when she had left the house, and then... The sound of metal clashing with metal and the sight of her brother and Mr. Darcy engaged in battle had frightened her.

"Elizabeth?" Jane touched her shoulder to alert her sister to her presence before carefully taking a seat next to her on the ground. She wrapped her arms around Elizabeth's shoulders. "Papa told me what happened."

"When will I learn to hold my tongue?" Elizabeth shook her head. "If I had remained silent..."

"Shhh," Jane cooed. "What has been done is done. We cannot alter that now."

"I love him, Jane. I love him most ardently."

Jane squeezed her close.

"This is my fault. If I had not allowed my anger to overcome me, William would not have said what he did, and Mr. Darcy would not have left me."

"William was wrong," Jane said firmly. "I will not excuse your actions, but I will also not allow you to bear all of this on yourself. You may have been demanding, and you may have spoken in anger. However, none of that would have happened if William had been reasonable."

Jane always had a way of framing a picture as it should be when Elizabeth was beginning to scramble the pieces and create scenarios that were less than accurate as her mind spun in its distress and struggled to right whatever cart had been upset.

"Papa said that Mr. Darcy has not given you up completely." Jane drew and released a deep breath. In it, Elizabeth could hear the weight of concern Jane bore. "We have only to hope William will regain his senses soon, and I think he will."

"He is so stubborn," Elizabeth refuted.

"As are you," Jane said as she smoothed Elizabeth's hair behind her ear on the far side of her head where Jane's arm rested around her sister's shoulders. "He was greatly shaken when I saw him. I have never seen him so."

Elizabeth shrugged as if she did not care, even though she did. Her heart hurt because of the fracture that had occurred between her and her brother.

"Give him some time. He is not without sense. He will see reason. Papa will make certain he does."

Elizabeth sighed. She hoped it was true.

Jane removed her arm from around her sister, wrapping it instead around Elizabeth's arm and snuggling into her side. It was often how they would sit and tell stories to one another at night when they were younger. They still did it now, though not so often.

"Do you remember when William first arrived?" Jane asked.

Elizabeth nodded. "He was so big, and he scowled so much."

Jane laughed. "That is what you said. You looked up at him and said, 'you are very tall' which you followed with 'why do you not smile?'"

"And Papa explained to me what it meant for someone to die."

Jane nodded. "And you decided it was your duty to see William smile. The torment you caused him with your questions! 'Do you like apples, William? They are a very cheery fruit. Do you like horses, William? I like riding with Papa. Would you like to have my kitten? She is very good at catching mice and at snuggling with me when I am afraid of the thunder.'"

Elizabeth laughed. "I was a trying child, was I not?"

"Excessively," Jane agreed. "And yet, you became the sister William loves best. No matter how you teased him about his incorrect sums or how often you followed him around when he had told you to stay home." She laughed softly again. "Do you remember falling in the stream? I think you were about eight, were you not?"

Elizabeth nodded. "I was, and that water was not warm."

"You had been told to stay home, but you wished to fish with William and his friends, who thought it great fun to challenge you to stand on a rock in the middle of the stream."

"On one foot," Elizabeth added.

"And you did it for about five seconds before falling into the water."

"William fished me out and wrapped me in his jacket."

"And proceeded to earn himself a black eye and a bloody nose venting his displeasure on his friends because they had caused you harm," Jane finished the story quietly. "He loves you. He acted foolishly, but he did it because it was you. He did not challenge Mr. Bingley."

Elizabeth dried her eyes again. She knew it was true. William was a determined protector of all his sisters, but he was downright immovable when it was anything that threatened her. When she was ill, it was he who would sit beside her bed reading or who would fetch tea and broth as needed. He had held her hand when the surgeon had stitched up the gash on her leg from another of her escapades when she had been following him without his permission. She could still see the ashen sheen of his face as she bit her lip to keep from crying out with each poke. He had made her look at him when her curiosity begged her to watch the gruesome work of the surgeon. And he had, after he had seen she was well, emptied the contents of his stomach.

"He means well, Lizzy."

"I know," Elizabeth admitted. "But he is wrong."

Jane rested her head on Elizabeth's shoulder. "And he will move the heavens above to correct his wrong for he will not be parted from you for anything in the world."

Elizabeth hoped with all her heart that it was true, for though she longed to see Mr. Darcy again and eventually be his wife, she knew that she would never be truly happy if it came at the expense of an irreparable breach between her and her brother.

They sat in silence for some time. Elizabeth's tears had finally stopped – or nearly had. There were a few that insisted on filling her eyes whenever she would think of either William or Mr. Darcy.

"Are you ready to go home?" Jane asked.

Elizabeth nodded. "I believe I am."

Jane rose first and helped Elizabeth up.

"What does Mama know?" Elizabeth asked as they began the walk back to Longbourn.

"She heard everything Papa told me, and she has

instructed that a bath be waiting for you as well as a cup of tea and a piece of toast."

"Am I to be confined to my bed?"

Jane nodded her head. "You know Mama. She would take to her bed, and therefore, it is expected that you will as well. However, that will likely be for the best, as you will not need to see William, nor will you have to hear Mama's moans over the situation, for I am certain I will be assigned to your care."

Elizabeth smiled. "I am sorry to be such a burden to you."

"You are never a burden, my dearest sister."

"Unless I have angered William and caused Mr. Bingley not to be allowed to call," Elizabeth teased.

"Well, yes, there is that," Jane agreed with a small laugh. "Perhaps that should be how we pass our time – teaching you how to hold your tongue." She pulled Elizabeth close. "I own that it is a fault and needs correction, but I love you just as you are, you know."

"I know, and I love you. However, I do not think I will need much instruction. If I can remember this day and the way my heart hurts for those I love, it will be enough."

"He loves you. Mr. Darcy, that is," Jane said. "Papa told me before I left to come to you about how he promised to wait for you and that he cried." She sighed. "You must admit that that is very romantic."

"Jane!"

"I know, the rest of the story is not pleasant, but to be loved so dearly." She sighed again. "I almost wish William had challenged Mr. Bingley."

"You do not," Elizabeth said with a laugh. Jane could be just as given to fanciful notions as Lydia at times.

Jane shrugged. "Perhaps I do not, but I would adore having a gentleman be so moved at the thought of losing me even for a short time."

Elizabeth shook her head. "You are impossible at times," she chided playfully, but she would not have Jane any other way, and she was excessively thankful for such a whimsical conversation that would put her in better spirits before she was to face her mother's sighs and lamentations before being tucked into bed.

Chapter 15

For two days, Darcy hid himself away in his room. The first day, he was accompanied by a bottle from Bingley's wine cellar. It had imparted the numbing stupor he sought for a time. He had felt blissfully separated from the real world and its woes until he awoke the next morning. Then, just as he knew it would, the world crashed in upon him in loud, nauseating waves, pounding at his head, and churning his stomach.

On the third day, Darcy arose and prepared him-self for the day. He would not wallow in misery for another day. Elizabeth was not lost to him forever, just for now, and his friend had need of his advice about accounts and crops and other such things. He would find a purpose – something into which he could throw himself, and in so doing, he hoped to be able to weather the time between now and when the younger Mr. Bennet finally located his senses and welcomed him with something a touch friendlier than a fencing foil.

"Good morning," Caroline greeted as Darcy entered the breakfast room. "I trust you are feeling much improved today."

He gave her a small smile. "I am, thank you." He poured some tea and took a seat.

"I visited Longbourn yesterday," Caroline continued.

Darcy took a sip of his tea and braced himself for what he assumed would be another attempt to sway him to her cause now that she knew Miss Elizabeth was not to be his for some time since Bingley had shared with her all that had happened.

"I called on Mr. William Bennet."

Darcy lifted a brow, curious to know why she had called on the gentleman.

"He was not home."

"Indeed?"

She nodded. "He left Longbourn the same day he met with you in the field."

"Why did you call on him?" Darcy was interested in the fact that Mr. William Bennet had not been home, but at the moment, he was more interested in why Caroline would be calling on him in the first place.

"To prove that my cap is no longer set at you." She lifted her chin and held his gaze.

"And it is set at Mr. William Bennet?" Darcy asked in confusion.

"Oh, goodness, no!" She laughed and then stopped suddenly as if captured by a thought. "I suppose he might not be so bad a catch." Her head tipped to the side as if she were considering the idea for the first time. "He is tall and, though not particularly handsome, he is not dreadful to look upon." She shrugged. "Many ties between families is often better than just one."

"You will have to explain that," Darcy said, lowering his cup and reaching for a scone. The cook at Netherfield was no slouch. Her work was delightful, and her scones were quickly becoming Darcy's favourites.

"You shall marry his sister. Charles will marry his other sister. And then, if I marry him, we shall all be tied together in several different strands. A nice tight knot."

"You would marry him just to complete some

knot of relations?" Darcy was still not certain he followed her logic.

Caroline shrugged again. "I would prefer not to, I believe, now that I have spoken about it. I do not think I could manage to keep my composure if I were to be too tightly tied to either Mrs. Bennet or her youngest daughters. I am not disparaging. I am simply declaring we do not get on well. Not to mentions, there is a noticeable lack of shops in Meryton."

Darcy nodded. He could not see Caroline tolerating Mrs. Bennet or a lack of shopping for any extended period of time.

"Then why did you call on him?" Darcy asked.

"I wished to share with him what I knew of Mr. Wickham. Mr. Wickham did attempt to flirt with me when we first met him, but I was too cunning to be drawn in."

"He did?"

She smiled at him and nodded. "Some gentlemen find both me and my inheritance attractive."

"I have never said you were unattractive," Darcy countered.

"No, you have not, but then you have not fallen for my charms either." She refilled her cup and settled back in her chair. "I thought if I could convince him of Mr. Wickham's rakish ways, I could perhaps do you a service." Her gaze fell to study the contents of her cup. "You are a friend, and even if that is all you shall ever be, I do not wish to see you suffer as you must have been – indeed, as you likely still are."

"I thank you for your kindness," he said. He would overlook the small amount of pleasure that seemed to fill her voice as she spoke of his suffering. He had disappointed her, and such feelings of satisfaction that the person who had disappointed you was suffering somewhat of the pain that he had caused were not unusual. He was thankful that she had been able to rise above those vengeful feeling to attempt to help him. If she had acted so thoughtfully more often, perhaps he would have considered her more closely. He paused before indulging in another bite of his scone. "I am still not choosing you."

She shrugged. "I know, but one cannot fault a lady for the attempt." When she smirked, she looked very much like her twin. "Truly," she continued, "I have given you up. I am not so foolish as to attempt to come between you and Miss Elizabeth. Truly."

"Thank you."

"Mr. Darcy."

Darcy looked up at the butler.

"When you are finished, sir, you have a visitor."

Darcy's brows furrowed. "Who might that be?"

"Mr. William Bennet, sir."

Darcy could not contain his look of surprise. He expected the young man to come to his senses at some point, but he had not thought it would be so soon. He had seemed more reticent in personality than to easily capitulate.

"Will you see him, sir? He was concerned you would not."

With good reason. "As soon as I have finished, I will join him in the front drawing room."

"Very good, sir. I am certain he will be most appreciative."

"You are not rushing?" Caroline asked as Darcy settled back into his chair to enjoy the last of his tea and scone at a leisurely pace.

"I think allowing him to cool his heels for a while might be best."

This reply was met with an approving smile.

"Would you like to join me for this?" he asked Caroline when he had finished his last morsel of food and drained his second cup of tea.

She sighed. "I do enjoy a good spat, but no. I will allow you the privacy you deserve."

He thanked her and went to find Mr. William Bennet.

"Mr. Darcy." William shot to his feet when Darcy entered the room.

"Mr. Ben –" Darcy's greeting stopped abruptly as he took in the condition of the gentleman before him. William appeared to be wearing the same clothes he had been wearing on the morning of their appointment, and they were exceedingly rumpled. However, that was not what arrested Darcy's words. No, that honour went to the state of the man's face. His right eye was nearly swollen closed, and his lower lip was two times the size it should be with a nasty gash held together by two stitches near the right corner of his mouth.

"Please forgive my appearance and my early call." He fiddled with what remained of his hat. "But I knew that if I were to go home first, Mother would not allow me to leave once she saw me."

"I can see why." Darcy motioned for him to retake his seat, which he did.

"I have been to town." He paused and looked at his hat. "I should have gone to town before now."

"I apologize, but I do not understand."

William blew out a breath and rose from his seat. "My father died when I was ten. That is when I came to live at Longbourn."

"I know. Your sister told me."

He paced in front of the windows behind the chair where he had been sitting. "What she likely did not tell you is that I thought I would never again have a reason to smile. I thought that my world had come to an end. My father was no pillar of exemplary behavior, but he was my father. He had told me about his unreasonable cousin and his wife who only had daughters. He had thought it humorous that they would be at my mercy when I came into my inheritance. I had no reason to not believe what he had told me about them, and so, I arrived at Longbourn expecting to be reviled and treated poorly."

"But you were not."

He shook his head. "No, I was welcomed with great comforting arms and by one impish young lady determined to see me smile." His lips attempted to tip up into a smile, though it was difficult with the lower one being so swollen. "Lizzy latched onto me and followed me around like a lost pup might do someone who fed it." He shook his head. "She was a lovely little bothersome shadow."

"And she stole your heart."

William nodded. "I would do nearly anything to protect any of the Bennets, but for Lizzy, I would do so much more. And I confess that desire clouded my judgment of you. For that, I must apologize."

Darcy gave him a small nod of his head. He could understand that sentiment. He was much the same when it came to those he loved.

William took his seat once again. "I went to town in search of Wickham. I now have in my possession nearly the full, truthful story of your relationship. There was a portion he would not tell me, no matter how much I insisted. He only said he could not because it would put his life in danger." Again, his lips attempted to tip into a smile. "More danger than it was in as I was asking him. I guess he knew I would not hang to know a secret." He met Darcy's eyes and held them with a knowing look. "I assume it is about your sister, and I will ask no further."

"Thank you, and it is. She was not ruined, but it was close."

William shook his head. "I have been an unmitigated arse."

"I will not refute that," Darcy agreed.

William chuckled. "You could not. Your character would not allow you to lie in such a fashion." He shifted uneasily. "I know I have no right to ask this, but there is something that I would very much like for you to do for me."

Darcy's brows rose. The fellow expected a favor?

"Elizabeth refuses to speak to me or even see me, and not without justification, as I have said, I was an arse. However, I do believe she might forgive me for my stupidity more easily if you were to accompany me to Longbourn." He blew out a breath. "There is no gentleman of more noble character with whom I would see her, for I know that from what I have heard, you will protect her as fiercely as I would, and that is all I have ever hoped for her to find in a husband."

Darcy smiled. "I would be delighted to be of service to you in such a fashion."

"Mr. Darcy."

Darcy turned to the butler.

"Your cousin and sister are here to see you, but I told then you were occupied."

"We are finished, are we not?" Darcy asked William. "I was about to ride out with Mr. Bennet, but I believe I can welcome my cousin and sister first while my horse is readied."

"Of course," William muttered as he fidgeted with his hat once again.

Darcy rose along with William and made all the proper introductions when Richard and Georgiana entered the room.

A sound as if the wind had been knocked out of him emanated from William, causing him to be only able to stammer a greeting and Darcy to chuckle. It was similar to how Darcy had felt when first introduced to William's sister. A Bingley William might not be, but anyone who would take Wickham in hand – quite literally – as William had for his sister was not a man Darcy would brush aside – even if that gentleman had caused a great deal of distress with his foolishness.

"You will have to excuse Mr. Bennet's appearance." Darcy motioned for them all to be seated.

"He has just come from extracting his displeasure on a fellow whose lies caused his sister some grief."

Richard, who had been looking at William, turned quickly to Darcy with a questioning look.

"Colonel, Miss Darcy!" Bingley cried as he entered the room. "Good heavens what happened to you?" he said as he took in the appearance of William. "This is not Darcy's doing, is it?"

Darcy laughed. "No. I have not laid one finger on Mr. Bennet."

"Though he would be well within his rights if he did," William added.

"I am confused," Georgiana said. "Why would my brother wish to harm Mr. Bennet?"

William blew out a breath and shook his head. "Because I was a fool and listened to a tale about your brother that was not true. However, I chose to believe it and was less than willing to allow him to be accepted by my sister."

Georgiana's eyes grew wide. "I beg your pardon? My brother has made an offer to someone?"

"I have," Darcy answered. Joy swelling in his heart at the admission.

"You have?" Richard nearly shouted.

"Yes, I have and so has Bingley," Darcy replied,

attempting to shift some of the attention from himself.

"Both of you?" Richard began to laugh. "I had heard tell that there were some beauties in the area, but so soon?"

"They are the most beautiful ladies in Hertfordshire," William's voice held a decided edge to it.

Darcy chuckled silently. Not even a colonel would be tolerated to even hint at disrespecting William's sisters.

"He does not exaggerate," Bingley replied.

"Well, I am happy for you, but I thought that I was needed to convince someone of Darcy's worth."

"That would be me," William said. "I need no further convincing. I believe I know all I need to know." He rubbed the area below his swollen lip. "I had a discussion with the fellow who lied to me, and after some *persuasion*, he told me the truth."

Richard leaned back, folded his arms, and smiled approvingly at William. "I do hope the other fellow looks at least as damaged as you do."

William's lips curled into a smile as best they could and said, "I have very few injuries comparatively."

To which Richard responded by calling William a fine fellow. Then he shook his head. "Then I am unneeded? There is nothing with which you require my assistance."

"Oh, no!" William said quickly. "There is an assembly next week, and there seems to never be enough gentlemen to dance with the ladies." He shrugged. "And I would like for once not to have to listen to my sisters complain about being left standing and not being able to dance every set."

"An assembly, you say?" Richard rubbed his chin. "I do like to dance, and since it is a country assembly, we might even allow Georgiana to attend, mightn't we?" He looked at Darcy hopefully.

"She is not out yet," Darcy answered.

"But it is a country assembly, and your betrothed will be there, will she not?"

"Yes," William replied, "and her four sisters. Three of whom have not yet been spoken for."

"You would throw your sisters at him, yet refuse Darcy?" Bingley asked.

"I have heard everything I need to know about Colonel Fitzwilliam," William replied with a smirk. "The fellow I spoke to and who blackened my eye has a healthy fear of the man, and that is a good enough recommendation for me."

"He should fear me," Richard muttered.

"Who?" Georgiana asked. "You all seem to know who this fellow is, and I would like to know."

"No," Darcy answered. "You would not."

"I am certain I would," she replied.

Darcy shook his head.

"He is not worth your notice," William replied. "A total scoundrel."

"Aye," Bingley agreed. "That he is." He clapped his hands together. "Have you been shown to your rooms?"

"No," Georgiana answered.

"Then, that must be done." Bingley turned to Darcy. "Shall we make it a grand party which calls at Longbourn today?"

Darcy smiled and clapped William on the shoulder. "We are going to Longbourn now. Apparently, William would like my help in persuading his sister to speak to him."

Bingley laughed. "As if she will notice more than you." He waved toward the door. "While Darcy is off courting his lady, allow me to make you comfortable by directing you to your rooms."

"Shall we?" Darcy asked William. "You might not be anxious to see your sister, but I will not lie. I am."

Darcy gathered his hat and coat, and then, the two men stepped out into the bright light of the day, both happy to be on their way to Longbourn. One hopeful to be forgiven, and the other to put his short agonizing wait to an end.

Chapter 16

Elizabeth knocked on the door to her father's study before opening it. "You wished to see me?"

"No," her father replied with a smile. "But William does, and I did not expect you to come if I told you that." He rose from his chair and crossed the room. "I think I shall go torment your mother's nerves for a while." He stopped in front of her and took her by the shoulders. "You are not to leave this room until this is settled." His lips curled up on one side in a small smirk. "And I have no doubt that it will be settled soon." He kissed her cheek and left the room.

"Lizzy?" William, who had been sitting in front of his father's desk, rose and turned toward her.

Elizabeth gasped, and her hand flew to her mouth. Whatever sharp welcome she had thought to give him died on her lips.

"I have heard the whole ugly truth – or as much of it as I could extract – from Mr. Wickham. I know you said I should hear it from Mr. Darcy, but..." he stopped talking and looked at the floor.

"But what?" Elizabeth questioned as she crossed to him. She gently touched his eye. "Does it hurt?"

"Not as much as my lip or my heart." He took her hand.

"Why did you not go to Mr. Darcy?" Elizabeth asked again.

"Because he was not the cause of my blindness to reason. Mr. Wickham was, and since I could not thrash myself for having caused you pain, I thought I might be able to thrash him and receive my just dues in the process."

"William!" Elizabeth scolded. "When will you stop censuring and calling out every gentleman who appears to do me harm? You did call him out, did you not?"

William nodded. "But, instead of swords, we met with only our hands as weapons, and not in a field. We met at a club where gentlemen tend to do this sort of thing for sport."

"You men are a funny lot," Elizabeth muttered.

"I will never stop protecting you, Lizzy," he

added. "At least not until that responsibility falls on another." He sighed and dropped her hand. "I do not feel worthy of your forgiveness. I have been an utter fool." He shook his head and rolled his eyes upward. "Likely the greatest fool in all of England."

"You were foolish," Elizabeth agreed. "But, you know the truth about Mr. Darcy now?"

"Mostly. Wickham would not tell me part of why he was attempting to tarnish Darcy's name, but I know about his dissipate behaviour and his refusal of the living, as well as his attempt to later claim it. You were correct. There were reasons for the refusal. I should have bowed to your greater abilities to reason things, but I was so determined to make certain you were not tying yourself to someone of questionable character that I convinced myself you were only protesting because he was handsome and rich." He grimaced as she glared at him. "Yes, that was ill-thought-out."

"Indeed."

He should know better than to think so of her. She had often told him and Jane that she would not marry any gentleman whom she did not feel she could respect, or whom she thought would not respect her. Admiration was longed for, of course, and wealth could not be ignored, but it was the character of a gentleman which would recommend him most strongly to her.

"All my thinking was rather faulty." He was looking at the floor once again. "And I should be very sorry if such foolishness has created a breach of a permanent nature between us."

"You hurt me." Elizabeth placed a hand on his cheek, causing him to look at her. "Not just by separating me from Mr. Darcy, whom I love, but by not valuing my judgment."

He leaned his cheek into her hand as a tear slid from his swollen eye. "I know. I have buffeted myself in spirit most severely for two days for that."

"You will not do it again?"

He sighed. "I shall attempt not to, but I cannot promise success."

"It is good enough." She removed her hand from his cheek and opened her arms to him in invitation. "You are forgiven."

He wrapped her in his large arms, crushing her against him, and thanked her over and over.

"I was not certain if you would forgive me," he

said when he released her. "So, I brought something with me that might help ensure my success."

She looked around the room, but she did not see any gifts.

"It is not in here," he said. "He is in the garden, waiting to see you."

Her hand flew to her heart as a smile spread across her face. "He? Mr. Darcy? Is Mr. Darcy here?"

William nodded his head. "I went to beg his forgiveness before I came home. I was fearful that Mother would not allow me out of her sight once she saw me."

"Has she seen you?"

"No, I came through the servant's entrance, and I intend to wash and put on fresh clothes before she does."

Elizabeth chuckled. "That will help you some, but not completely." Their mother was not one to take an injury to any of her children with any amount of composure. A wound to one of her children was always the most severe of that sort she had ever seen.

"I have already obtained all the potions and tinctures she will require," he added. "Now, while I sneak upstairs to make myself somewhat presentable to our mother, you should escape to the garden."

Elizabeth threw her arms around him. "Though you are a fool at times, I could not ask for a better brother. I love you and am so happy I will not have to be parted from you, for I would still choose Mr. Darcy."

He squeezed her tightly and then released her. "I am glad to hear it. I should not want any of my sisters to choose me over their husbands. Now, go. And when you are done in the garden, if you could distract Mother with Mr. Darcy, I would appreciate it greatly. She will be more forgiving of my stupidity if she knows I have made amends in such a fashion."

Elizabeth tipped her head. "Perhaps I will, or perhaps I will send Mr. Darcy home, so that you can suffer as you should."

"You said you forgave me," he reminded her.

"Yes, and I will not withdraw that, but there are consequences to all actions, are there not?"

"Please, Lizzy," he begged.

She said not a word in reply, choosing instead to only smile and shrug before leaving the room.

She was happy to have their relationship restored, and she was nearly positive she would invite Mr. Darcy in just so she could have him near for longer. However, she was not above enjoying making her brother feel uneasy for just a while longer.

~*~*~

Mr. Darcy was waiting for her.

The thought made her smile as she put on her pelisse, and it caused her breath to catch as she saw him, pacing a circuit at the far end of the garden nearest the servant's entrance. It was a portion of the garden that could not be seen from the sitting room. William must have either been hiding Mr. Darcy from their mother, or he wished to give her a private place to be reunited with Mr. Darcy. Whatever his motivation might have been, she was glad that Mr. Darcy was here where they could speak in private.

He turned toward her just at that moment, and a beautiful smile spread across his face. A smile that was just for her and because of her. Jane was right. It was very romantic to have a gentleman respond to you in such a demonstrative fashion.

"It has been a long two days," he said as she approached him.

"It has," she agreed.

He extended his arm to her. "Would you care to take a turn around the garden?"

She placed her hand on his arm but shook her head. "There is a bench to our right. I would rather sit there." There she would be guaranteed of not being interrupted by some sister being sent out by their mother to act as a chaperone.

"If that is what you prefer." He led her down the short path to the bench. "I was surprised to see your brother this morning. I had thought it would be longer before he came to see me."

Elizabeth allowed him to pull her close as they sat down. "I was surprised as well, though I should not be, I suppose."

"He cares for you very much," Darcy said, putting words to Elizabeth's thoughts.

"He does."

"He is not the only one who cares for you," Darcy lifted her fingers and kissed them. "Will you still have me? Even after I walked away from you?"

"You have no need to apologize," she chided. "Your actions were beyond reproach. I, on the other hand, was once again demanding and that caused the whole ordeal. William would not have made his demand as he did if I had not provoked him. Of course, I would not have provoked him if he had not challenged you, so the beginnings of the wrong lie with him. However, I am still at fault."

He placed a finger on her lips. "Will you still have me?"

She nodded, and he removed his finger from her lips. "If you will still have me."

"I cannot imagine living without your demanding person at my side. Two days without you was enough." He wrapped an arm around her and pulled her closer to him. "I love you, Elizabeth. I do not know how you stole my heart so quickly, but you have. And I do not want it back. Keep it and care for it for now and always."

She rested her head against his shoulder right above where she could hear his heart beating. It was a wonderful, reassuring sound. "Seeing as you have my heart, it seems only proper that I keep yours in return." She took his free hand and held it between both of hers. "I love you, though, like you, I do not know how it happened so quickly, but this closeness we share feels as if it has always been."

"Perhaps that is how it is supposed to be."

"Perhaps," she agreed.

They sat as they were, her head resting against his shoulder while she held his hand, for several minutes.

"William is hoping I will invite you in so that Mama will be too happy to be put out with him. She was very displeased when Papa told her about him challenging you and demanding I chose you or him."

Darcy laughed. "I can imagine any mother would be upset with a son for driving away a suitor."

"Seeing us well-married is my mother's sole goal in life aside from having her dinner parties spoken about for longer than her sister's ever are."

"I shall remember that and praise her when I can. It is best for a gentleman to keep his mother-in-law happy, or so my father said."

Elizabeth giggled. She would enjoy continuing to learn about him. "Well, then, I suppose I must invite you in and not just because I do not wish to have you ever leave me again."

They rose reluctantly from the comfort of their secluded spot in the garden.

"I am not returning you to the house without a kiss and a promise that you will not suffer me to wait too long before we marry." He wrapped her in his embrace.

"I had hoped you would kiss me," she admitted, tipping her face up to look at him and meet his lips as they descended to hers.

There would be three months to wait for the wedding, but as Darcy and Elizabeth waited, this corner of the garden, as well as Elizabeth's favourite tree on the knoll, would know many of their secrets and witness many ardent kisses such as this one. And with each meeting, whether it was on the knoll, in a drawing room, or on a dance floor, Elizabeth would find herself delighted by the love that she found and was constantly reminded of as she began the lifelong pleasure of learning about the man who held her now.

William would be sorry to see her leave Longbourn. However, in a year's time, he would find his way to London to spend a season with the sister he loved best in all the world while he sought to prove himself worthy of a brother's good opinion while hoping that brother would prove to be far less foolish than he had been while assessing Mr. Darcy.

Confounding Caroline
Excerpt

If you enjoyed this unique take on how Darcy and Eliz-
abeth found their happily ever after, then you might
enjoy my Marrying Elizabeth Series which follows our
dear couple's journey from the first acknowledgment of
feelings through several obstacles as their love grows on
their way to happily ever after. The first obstacle which
must be overcome is Caroline Bingley. The story of how
that all unfolds can be found in book one, Confounding
Caroline. The first chapter of this story can be found
below.

CHAPTER 1

Fitzwilliam Darcy handed his coat and beaver to
his friend's butler, while that friend, Charles Bingley, leaned nonchalantly against the sitting room's
door frame. The soft glow of a lamp, which

remained lit, shone behind him, indicating that Bingley had been engaged in some activity in the room before which he now stood.

"I had hoped you would be home, but I did not expect it," Darcy said in greeting. It was not Bingley's normal wont to remain at home. "Reading?" he queried with some surprise as he took note of the book in Bingley's hand.

Bingley shrugged. "I do read on occasion."

"I would not wish to keep you from your amusements." Darcy smirked slightly. If he knew his friend, Bingley would likely not mind the disruption since Bingley preferred people to books.

Bingley shook his head and chuckled. "Come, my study would be more comfortable than the sitting room and less likely to be invaded by females should Caroline return early."

"I am surprised you did not accompany her to the Grahams' soiree," Darcy said as he followed Bingley into the study.

"I have had my fill of ferrying Caroline around only to have her turn up her pert little nose at every gentleman she meets, so I sent her with Louisa and Hurst."

He tucked his book away on a shelf behind his

desk, and then opening the door on the right side of his desk, he pulled out a bottle of amber coloured liquid and two glasses.

"I find I tire of society. It is always the same. The same ladies in different dresses with different coloured hair and hats, but the same gossip, the same weather, the same pleasantries. It's just so much of the same, over and over and over and over." He handed a glass to Darcy and smiled. "Besides, if I am not mistaken, I will not be the only one who will enjoy this Caroline-free evening."

Darcy chuckled "The quiet is agreeable to me, but you have never enjoyed silence so much as I." There was something different about Bingley the past few weeks. He did not smile as much as was his usual wont, and he seemed to tuck himself away in his study more and more. Darcy swirled the liquid in his glass and threw one leg over the other. The leather squeaked as he shifted in the chair across from Bingley.

Bingley sighed. "I find I am longing for the country, but Caroline will hear nothing of leaving town when there are so many functions to attend." He took a draught from his glass. "If I thought she meant to find a husband, trotting her around to the various venues might not be so bothersome, but she is not intent on snaring anyone but you."

Darcy knew that fact very well. Caroline had never been reserved in demonstrating her preference for him over every gentleman she met. "A title and a larger fortune might dissuade her."

The hint of bitterness in Bingley's laugh surprised Darcy almost as much as Bingley's wishing to leave town and avoid society. These were not Bingley actions. They were behaviours that were more likely to be attributed to Darcy rather than his gregarious friend.

"She is as stubborn as a mule," Bingley muttered, "and almost as bright."

Darcy's brows rose. He was not surprised by the fact that Bingley was complaining about his sister. He had heard Bingley complain about Caroline before — many times. However, he had never heard Bingley complain about anything more than her incessant need to purchase fripperies and dresses or the way she nattered on about this person or that. There was something decidedly wrong with his friend, and Darcy had a sinking feeling that he knew just what it was.

"You surprise me," Darcy said, not wishing to

broach the topic of the cause of the change in Bingley but knowing it was necessary. "Was it not you who claimed to be happy wherever you were, be it town or country?"

"That was before," Bingley said over the rim of his glass.

"Before what?" Darcy prodded.

"Before I took an estate." Bingley shifted in his chair uneasily, studying the painting above the fireplace for a few moments before allowing his attention to return to his friend. He sighed deeply as his gaze fell to where Darcy's foot slowly bounced up and down.

Surreptitiously, Darcy glanced at his friend. He recognized Bingley's sigh, for it was the same groan of uncertainty that had taken up residence in his own chest. It was a new and unwelcome feeling, and it was not something that, though he had tried, he could command away. He had not been able to erase it with busyness, nor had he been able to wash it away with drink. There remained only one option for dealing with such uncertainty and its pretty reason. It must be acknowledged for what it was. The root of it must be exposed, then left to wither away with time — at least, for him. For his friend, he hoped for a different outcome.

"Is it the estate or the society in Hertfordshire that you miss, my friend?" Darcy's voice was quiet, and he fixed his eyes on the wall beyond Bingley's head. A small smile played at his mouth as he contemplated the image of smiling eyes and an impertinent grin that always came to his mind when he thought of Hertfordshire. "Netherfield seems like a fine estate, and the neighbourhood was not without its enchantments." He sipped his drink and then swirled it again, watching the liquid swirl up the sides of the glass.

"I thought you loathed the inhabitants of Hertfordshire." Bingley's voice was filled with incredulity. "Is that not why you and my sisters were so hasty in joining me in town — the people are beneath us, there is no society worth keeping, that sort of thing?

Again, Darcy's brows rose at the rancor in Bingley's voice. He sighed heavily, and colour crept up his cheeks. This would not be a pleasant discussion.

"I did not loathe all of the inhabitants. I found some of them to be quite delightful — so delightful, in fact, that leaving seemed safer than staying." He rose and walked to the window. Admitting his folly and weakness would be easier if he were able to move about and not have to face the friend whom he had, he suspected, unknowingly injured.

Bingley drummed his fingers on the arm of his chair and raised a brow in anticipation of an expected explanation.

"She is here in town." Darcy placed his empty glass on a side table and allowed his eyes to remain on it rather than look at his friend.

"Who is here in town?"

Darcy drew a deep breath and spared Bingley only a glance before returning his gaze to his glass. "Miss Bennet."

"Miss Bennet?"

Darcy nodded.

"How do you know?" Bingley was on his feet and pacing. "Have you seen her?"

Darcy shook his head and sighed. "No, I have not seen her, but your sisters have." He turned once again toward the window. Bingley's reaction to the news was as expected and proved to Darcy how deeply attached his friend was to Miss Bennet.

"My sisters?" Bingley stood beside his friend, his brows drawn together in question.

Darcy turned toward him. "This afternoon, while you were out, I came by to drop off those papers." He pointed to the packet sitting unopened on the somewhat cluttered desk. "Caroline informed me that Miss Bennet had called."

"She was here? Miss Bennet was here?" Bingley's eyes were wide with astonishment. "Why did Caroline not tell me?"

Darcy wished to walk away from his friend, so that he could not see the pain in Bingley's eyes, but he would not. "It seems your sister is actively trying to separate you and Miss Bennet. She seemed to think I would be impressed by her belittling of the inferior society of the country." He paused and drew a deliberate breath. "At one time I would have agreed with her, but I no longer do."

Bingley crossed his arms and studied his friend.

Darcy winced under the examination, but it was not more than he deserved. Unable to bear both his shame and the scrutiny of his friend any longer, he turned back to the window. "I have to make a confession, Bingley. You may wish to throw me out of your home when I am finished, and I will fully understand if you do." Darcy continued to stare out the window, but he could feel the eyes of his friend boring into him.

"I wished to separate you from Miss Bennet when we left Hertfordshire." He closed his eyes as he heard his friend's muttered oath. "I told you she seemed indifferent to you. While it is true that I did not notice any particular regard for you on her part, it is not the reason I wished to separate you from her. It is not even the connection to her family or the supposed inferior society of Meryton that led me to take the actions I did." He swallowed and drew a deep fortifying breath before continuing. "I did not wish for you to become attached to Miss Bennet, for it would place me in an awkward situation. I was being completely and utterly selfish." He turned to look at his friend. "I am sorry," he whispered.

"An awkward situation?" Bingley wore a look of displeasure Darcy had rarely seen. "You would separate me from the woman I loved because it would somehow make your life awkward?"

Darcy nodded slowly. "Yes."

"Explain yourself," Bingley demanded, "for I do

not have the pleasure of understanding your meaning."

Darcy shrugged one shoulder. "I thought if we left, if you and Miss Bennet were not allowed to become attached, I could avoid the danger, but I have discovered that the danger is not confined to Hertfordshire. It has followed me here to town. It haunts me day and night." He turned back towards the window as he continued.

"I am expected to marry well, to make a match that will increase the wealth and position of my family. It is what my father and uncle have always taught me."

"You are still making no sense."

Darcy could hear the exasperation in his friend's voice. It was rather how he had felt since leaving Hertfordshire — annoyed, disturbed, and vexed by the memory of Miss Elizabeth Bennet.

"How would my being fortunate enough to marry a lady such as Miss Bennet," Bingley continued, "impose upon some imagined need of yours to marry a lady of wealth and standing?"

"Miss Bennet has sisters," Darcy said to the darkness of the night before him.

"Yes, four," Bingley retorted. "I still do not see —"

"But only one," Darcy interrupted, "with the musical laughter of a brook, eyes as expressive as any the masters have painted, and a mind that is..." he shook his head "so quick, so very quick and keen."

Darcy blew out a breath. "I imagined one day I would find a woman who would meet all the qualifications my uncle and father had taught me are necessary for the wife of a man of my standing and that we would eventually learn to esteem one another. But, I cannot fathom such a match after..." His voice trailed off.

A hand grasped his shoulder. "After meeting the one person you find you do not wish to live without." It was not a question that Bingley asked but rather a statement of deep understanding.

Darcy gave his friend a sad smile and nodded mutely.

"Now, you know why I am longing for the country," Bingley said softly.

Darcy nodded again. "I suspected as much. It is why I came here tonight — to discover if I was correct. I will not stand in your way. You deserve happiness. You have been a good friend to me, and I would not want to part for any other reason." Darcy turned to leave.

"What do you mean part?" Bingley asked. "I do not hate you for what you have done if that is what has you worried. I am not happy, but I am not angry. There is no reason for us to part."

Darcy stood with his hand on the doorknob. "I do not think I can bear hearing of her, especially when she belongs to another. It is just too much." His shoulders slumped. "You shall always remain my friend, Bingley. I will always be ready to serve you in any way, but please...please, do not ask me to be a witness to that."

Before You Go

If you enjoyed this book, be sure to let others
know by leaving a review.

~*~*~

Always know what's new with Leenie's books
by subscribing to her mailing list
and as a thank you, you will receive a copy of
Teatime Tales as well as *Better Than She Deserved, A
Willow Hall Romance Sequel*:
Book News from Leenie Brown
(http://eepurl.com/bSıeIı)

Acknowledgements

There are many who have had a part in the creation of this story. Some have read and commented on it. Some have proofread for grammatical errors and plot holes. Others have not even read the story and a few, I know, never will. However, their encouragement and belief in my ability, as well as their patience when I became cranky or when supper was late or the groceries ran low, was invaluable.

And so, I would like to say *thank you* to Zoe, Rose, Betty, Kristine, Ben, and Kyle as well as my patrons on Patreon. I feel blessed by your help, support, and understanding.

I have not listed my dear husband in the above group because, to me, he deserves his own special thank you, for, without his somewhat pushy insistence that I start sharing my writing, none of my writing goals and dreams would have been realized.

More Dash of Darcy and Companions Stories

Finally Mrs. Darcy

Waking to Mr. Darcy

A Very Merry Christmas (*A sequel to Waking to Mr. Darcy*)

Discovering Mr.Darcy

Not an Heiress (*A sequel to Discovering Mr. Darcy*)

Unravelling Mr. Darcy

Becoming Entangled (*A sequel to Unravelling Mr. Darcy*)

Enticing Miss Darcy (*A sequel to Becoming Entangled*)

Mr. Darcy's Comfort

Master of Longbourn (*A sequel to Mr. Darcy's Comfort*)

Other Leenie B Books

Novels ~ Novellas ~ Shorts

~*~

Oxford Cottage: A Pride and Prejudice Variation

For Peace of Mind: A Pride and Prejudice Variation

Teatime Tales: Six Short and Sweet Austen-Inspired Stories

Listen To Your Heart: A Pride and Prejudice Variation

With the Colonel's Help: A Pride and Prejudice Novella

~*~

Darcy Family Holidays
Two Days before Christmas (book 1)
One Winter's Eve (book 2)

~*~
The Choices Series: Pride & Prejudice Novellas
Her Father's Choice (book 1)
No Other Choice (book 2)
His Inconvenient Choice (book 3)
Her Heart's Choice (book 4)
~*~
Willow Hall Romances
And Then Love: A Pride and Prejudice Variation Prequel (book 1)
The Tenant's Guest: A Pride and Prejudice Variation Novella (book 2)
So Very Unexpected: A Pride and Prejudice Variation Novel (book3)
At All Costs: A Pride and Prejudice Variation Novel (book 4)
Better Than She Deserved: A Pride and Prejudice Novelette (sequel 1)
~*~
Touches of Austen Collection
His Beautiful Bea
~*~
Other Pens
Through Every Storm: A Pride and Prejudice Novella

Henry: To Prove Himself Worthy (*Mansfield Park, Episode 1*)
Charles: To Discover His Purpose (*Mansfield Park, Episode 2*)

About the Author

Leenie Brown has always been a girl with an active imagination, which, while growing up, was a both an asset, providing many hours of fun as she played out stories, and a liability, when her older sister and aunt would tell her frightening tales. At one time, they had her convinced Dracula lived in the trunk at the end of the bed she slept in when visiting her grandparents!

Although it has been years since she cowered in her bed in her grandparents' basement, she still has an imagination which occasionally runs away with her, and she feeds it now as she did then — by reading!

Her heroes, when growing up, were authors, and the worlds they painted with words were (and still are) her favourite playgrounds! Now, as an adult, she spends much of her time in the Regency world, playing with the characters from her favourite Jane Austen novels and those of her own creation.

When she is not traipsing down a trail in an attempt to keep up with her imagination, Leenie resides in the beautiful province of Nova Scotia with her two sons and her very own Mr. Brown (a wonderful mix of all the best of Darcy, Bingley, and Edmund with a healthy dose of the teasing Mr. Tilney and just a dash of the scolding Mr. Knightley).

Connect with Leenie Brown

E-mail:
LeenieBrownAuthor@gmail.com
Facebook:
www.facebook.com/LeenieBrownAuthor
Blog:
leeniebrown.com
Patreon:
https://www.patreon.com/LeenieBrown
Subscribe to Leenie's Mailing List:
Book News from Leenie Brown
(http://eepurl.com/bS1eI1)
Join Leenie on Austen Authors:
austenauthors.net